COUGAR'S FIRST CHRISTMAS

(Cascade Shifters #2)

Jessie Donovan

This book is a work of fiction. Names, characters, places, and incidents are either the product of the writer's imagination or are used fictitiously, and any resemblance to actual persons, living or dead, business establishments, events, or locales is entirely coincidental.

Cougar's First Christmas
Copyright © 2014 Laura Hoak-Kagey
Mythical Lake Press
First Edition

Cover Art by Clarissa Yeo of Yocla Designs.

ISBN 13: 978-1942211105

To My Friends & Family
Despite my hermit-like status at times,
you're still there for me

Other Books by Jessie Donovan

Stonefire Dragons
Sacrificed to the Dragon
Seducing the Dragon
Revealing the Dragons
Healed by the Dragon
Reawakening the Dragon
Loved by the Dragon
Surrendering to the Dragon
Cured by the Dragon

Lochguard Highland Dragons
The Dragon's Dilemma
The Dragon Guardian
The Dragon's Heart
The Dragon Warrior (Feb 2017)

Asylums for Magical Threats
Blaze of Secrets
Frozen Desires
Shadow of Temptation
Flare of Promise

Cascade Shifters
Convincing the Cougar
Reclaiming the Wolf
Cougar's First Christmas
Resisting the Cougar

Chapter One

Sean Fisher was putting the last few sprinkles on his slightly burnt, reindeer-shaped sugar cookies when his cell phone went off. He looked at the screen, saw it was his older sister, Danika, and clicked receive. "Hey, kitty cat, what's up?"

His sister growled over the line. "I'll make sure to call you kitten every chance I get if you ever let me meet your human girlfriend."

Sean glanced at the clock. "Introducing Lauren to a group of cougar-shifters is bad enough. Introducing her to you is like a nightmare."

"Hey, if she can't stand up to me, she doesn't deserve my baby brother. The Fisher family protects its own."

Despite having heard his sister say that sentence ten thousand times before, he still smiled. "Is there a reason you're calling? I have special plans for my female tonight, and you're kind of taking away time from my awesome preparations."

"I'm calling because I just heard through the grapevine about you meeting the human's parents tomorrow. Are you sure that's a smart idea? If this isn't serious, Sean, then don't risk both yourself and this Lauren woman, especially since Human Purity is looking for targets in the Seattle area."

Of course his sister had heard about his plans. Danika Fisher kept the pulse of the clan to such a degree he wouldn't be surprised if she knew everyone's darkest secrets.

Still, her concerns about Human Purity were valid. They were a group of religious and secular protesters who believed humans and shifters should be segregated. "Look, Dani, I'm twenty-five years old and I can take care of myself. You're the one who trained me as a teenager, after all. So unless you doubt your own skills, trust me for once."

"It's not a matter of trusting you, Sean. They're starting to kidnap shifters and make videos showing their torture and killings. One cougar-shifter doesn't stand a chance against a gang from Purity armed with tranquilizers."

"Of course I know that, Dani, but meeting her family tomorrow is important. I love Lauren Spencer with every cell in my body, and I want her to be my mate."

He hadn't meant for that secret to come out, but there it was.

The line went silent for a few seconds. Then Dani said, "Matings and marriages between shifters and humans are illegal, little brother."

He turned away from the sugar cookies on the kitchen counter and clenched his free hand. "I don't care. She's mine, and if I have to wait ten years for the law to change in order to make it official, then so be it."

"If that's what you want, then go for it. Just don't expect me to be all sugary nice when I first meet her. If she runs from me, then she's not worth the trouble or possible jail time, Sean."

While he was ninety-eight percent sure Lauren would do just fine with his sister and his clan, he wasn't about to let his sister know there was any doubt at all. "We'll see if you don't end up running from her. After all, she knows the correct dosages to knock a shifter unconscious before she pulls out all your teeth."

10

COUGAR'S FIRST CHRISTMAS

His sister snorted. "Only you could make being a dental student sound scary."

Smiling, Sean glanced to the clock. "I really need to go, Dani. Lauren will be here any minute. I'll call you after the Winter Celebration."

"Just be extra careful, Sean. And give a growl in greeting to your female."

He gave his sister a growl. "I threw it back at you instead. Bye, Dani."

He tossed the phone aside. His sister's warnings were valid, but Lauren's parents only lived about an hour from Seattle, in a city called Lakewood. Since they would be on I-5, the major freeway, almost the entire time, they would be fine.

Pushing his sister's worries aside, he took one last look around his small apartment to make sure everything was ready. Presents were wrapped under his very first, and somewhat lopsided, Christmas tree. Lauren's fuzzy, red and white stocking, which held his most important gift, was atop the coffee table since he didn't have a fireplace. Lights danced around the ceiling, reflecting off the glass snowflakes he'd found today at the last minute. And finally, his sugar cookies, made from a box mix, were decorated and waiting.

To him, it looked more like a Christmas bomb had exploded inside his apartment, but Lauren would like it.

Over the last six months, his female had done so much to accept his shifter ways, such as accepting him in cat-form and allowing him to scent-mark her apartment. So this was his way of trying to accept her human traditions. After all, shifters didn't celebrate Christmas, but rather held a winter celebration instead.

Since he fully intended to have Lauren as his mate, he needed to prove to her that he could make her happy. Giving her a great Christmas, her favorite holiday, was only the start.

Meeting her family tomorrow was just as important since it would allow her to see what she was getting into. Lauren was close to her family, and it would tear her apart if they didn't accept him.

His inner cougar growled at his uncertainty. *It will be fine. She is ours. She is strong.*

Pacing the living room, he realized his cougar was right. Over the last six months, they'd faced death threats and censure everywhere they went. Hell, just being his girlfriend and spending the night at his apartment could get her arrested.

Lauren wasn't a weak human. No, she had a hidden strength that both man and cougar admired.

Still, he was nervous. If tomorrow didn't go well and her family rejected him, she might leave him.

Stop it, asshole. Everything would be fine. His little human loved him, and damn it, he would try his best to ensure they had a future together.

~ ~ ~

Lauren Spencer pulled into the parking lot of Sean's apartment building and turned off the ignition. Glancing at the rearview mirror, she waited to see if the blue sedan that had been tailing her from the university would pull in after her. She counted to sixty, but no other cars pulled into the lot. She brushed off the car as coincidence.

COUGAR'S FIRST CHRISTMAS

Being paranoid sucked big-time, but her choice of boyfriend made her the target of some very dangerous people, such as Human Purity. And Purity had a hatred of shifters unlike anything since the Nazi's hatred of the Jews in World War II.

Not that she would trade Sean for anything. Just thinking about her boyfriend in his beautiful tan-furred and blue-eyed cougar form as she stroked his back, or the way he loved to nuzzle her neck while in human form before he kissed her, warmed Lauren's heart. How her blabbing during his emergency visit to her dental school six months ago, and asking to see his feline teeth no less, had led to this point in her life, she didn't know. But she had no regrets, and tomorrow she looked forward to finally introducing Sean to her parents and brother.

Realizing tomorrow was Christmas Eve, Lauren's thoughts about Human Purity vanished, and she felt a rush of giddiness. Ever since she'd been a child, Lauren had loved Christmas. Not because of receiving presents or stuffing her face at Christmas dinner, but because of the gathering of the family and all of their crazy traditions. No doubt her mother would have the same fifteen different types of cookies she made every year stashed in the freezer, off limits to everyone until Christmas Day. Not even her shifter boyfriend would be able to sneak one past her mother's careful watch.

She only hoped her mother liked Sean. If he were human, she'd be fine with it even though Sean was white and she was black, but shifters were a whole other group. Not everyone approved of their animal sides and believed them little better than beasts to be tamed.

Stop it, Lauren. Mom will love him like you do. Holding that thought close, Lauren exited the car with her duffel bag in hand, ascended the stairs to Sean's third floor apartment, and knocked.

13

A small part of her wished she had a key, but a key to a shifter's apartment could land her in jail. After all, they weren't legally supposed to live together. Some cops would look the other way, but Sean hadn't wanted to risk it. As such, they only spent the night together on special occasions, like tonight.

And she intended to make it count.

The lock clicked and Sean's head poked through the opening. Instead of inviting her in, he grinned at her, and she instantly grew suspicious. "Okay, what are you hiding?"

His look turned to one of mock innocence. "Who says I'm hiding anything?"

She poked his nose with her forefinger. "I know you, Sean Fisher, and you're hiding something. If you don't let me in, I'll just find somewhere else to sleep tonight and you'll miss out on my two Christmas presents for you."

"Presents?"

She couldn't help but smile as his cougar's curiosity shined out of his eyes. "Yep, both are one of a kind and are Lauren Spencer originals."

He started to open the door but then stopped as he shook his head. "No, I want to give you my surprise first since it's all set up. The instant you come inside, the surprise will be ruined. Close your eyes and I'll guide you. Then you can give me yours afterward."

Her heart skipped a few beats. She teased Sean for loving surprises, but she was no different.

Still, she knew her cougar-shifter well enough to clarify a few things. "This surprise doesn't involve a white coat, handcuffs, and a vibrator does it?"

14

Laughing, he held out a hand to her. "No, not this time. Now, give me your hand, baby. It's killing me to have you here and not show you my surprise."

Placing her hand in his, she grinned. "Well, someone has to keep your silly-ass antics in check."

Sean squeezed her hand and his touch sent a little thrill through her body. His hands were large and warm, and could be very naughty when the man put his mind to it.

Just last night, those fingers had made her come twice before he'd even thrust his cock inside her.

A whistle shattered her memory of last night's steamy sex. The instant she met his gaze again, Sean's eyes flashed cougar blue. His voice was low and husky when he said, "Whatever you're thinking about, stop it. If you become any wetter, I won't be able to focus long enough to do this properly."

Of course. She should know by now that Sean could scent when she was aroused. Although, she wasn't quite sure she'd call it a drawback...

She banished the images of Sean and his thick, naughty fingers and closed her eyes. "Okay, I'm ready. The sooner you give me my surprise, the sooner I can give you yours."

She heard a grunt, and then felt Sean tug her forward as he placed a hand on her lower back. After taking a few awkward steps, Sean moved his hand from her back to her neck and squeezed lightly. "Open your eyes, Lauren."

As soon as she opened her eyes, Lauren gasped. Sean's entire apartment was decked out for Christmas.

On the far side of the room, the lopsided Christmas tree was adorable, as was the haphazard way he'd hung the ornaments and the garland. Lights lined the ceiling, flashing in some kind of pattern that sparkled off the glass snowflakes hanging nearby.

There were even two giant, red stockings laying on the coffee table next to a stuffed Christmas bear. The plate of slightly burnt cookies in the shape of reindeers made her heart squeeze; Sean didn't cook often, but he'd attempted to make cookies for her.

Sean's voice filled her ears. "Well? How did I do?"

Turning back toward him, she said, "Oh, Sean. It's amazing."

Happiness flashed in his eyes and she couldn't resist putting her arms up to rest on either side of his neck. His arms instantly went around her waist, and his warmth and male scent surrounded her in that sense of comfort, safety, and love she always felt when her cougar held her close.

There was also no denying his thick, hard cock against her stomach. Yet more wetness rushed between her legs and Sean's nostrils flared as he said, "Lauren, I'm tempted to rip off your clothes right now."

Since he could extend his claws while in human form, she knew he wasn't bluffing.

As she caressed the skin at the back of his neck with one of her thumbs, she whispered, "Not before I give you one of my presents."

"Fuck your present. You're turned on and I need to take care of you."

That was a bonus she'd learned about shifters—they usually made sure their females orgasmed first.

"No." She stepped back and he let his arms fall with a growl. She smiled at the mix of understanding and possessiveness. "Stop pouting. I think you'll like what I have for you."

"Then hurry up. I want to fuck you at least three times before dinner."

Cougar's First Christmas

Heat flashed through her body and her nipples hardened at the image of Sean taking her against the wall, then over the table, and maybe in the shower. Her man always surprised her, and she loved him for it.

But tonight, it was her turn to surprise him.

She cleared her throat. "Wait here." She took two steps and then added, "And no peeking."

Crossing his arms over his broad, muscled chest, Sean grunted. "You have five minutes before I come find you."

She tried to frown but failed. "Believe me, it'll be worth it."

Sean's expression softened. "Baby, you're always worth it."

Her throat tightened with emotion. Rather than have her voice crack, she nodded, picked up the bag she'd brought with her, and rushed into the bathroom to change.

~ ~ ~

Sean struggled to think of anything but freeing his hard cock, which ached against the fly of his jeans. His female was wet and craving for his touch, and both man and cougar wanted nothing more than to ease it.

But she'd gone to some trouble to put together a surprise for him, so he contented himself with readjusting his dick to a slightly less uncomfortable position and waiting for her.

Exactly five minutes after she'd left, he heard the bathroom door open. His inner cougar's ear perked up. What had she done for them?

While his hearing wasn't as keen as a wolf's, it was good enough to hear the soft fall of Lauren's footsteps down the hall. A few seconds later, she appeared and stood in front of him.

17

Sean stopped breathing.

His female's breasts were covered by white lace, held up by thin straps that went around her neck. The contrast of Lauren's deep brown skin against the white lace all but begged him to kiss her soft skin, nuzzle her small, high breasts, and then relieve them of their lacey prison so he could suck her hard nipples into his mouth.

With great effort, he managed to move his gaze away from her nipples poking against the lace downward to see her shapely hips and thighs just visible through the red, semi-sheer material that stopped just past her pussy. If that wasn't enough, she had on white garters.

She was like a Christmas present that needed to be unwrapped.

Lauren cleared her throat and he forced his gaze back up to hers. "Well? Do you like it?"

Uncertainty danced in her eyes, and neither man nor cougar liked it. "I love it. But..."

"But what?"

He moved closer and traced the warm skin of her arm with his forefinger. "All I can think about is unwrapping you."

Her breath hitched, and he smiled. He moved his finger to her right breast and traced the edge where the white lace lay against her dark skin. With each pass, not only did her breathing speed up, the scent of her arousal grew stronger.

Yet he decided anticipation would make her come faster, so he moved a hand to her upper thigh and squeezed. "My beautiful human, let's see how wrapped up you are."

Before she could reply, he moved his right hand between her thighs. His fingers instantly came into contact with her pussy,

18

and a swipe of his fingers between her wet, swollen folds caused Lauren to grab his biceps as she let out a soft cry. "Sean."

Rubbing once more, Lauren moaned and he removed his hand, skimming it around her hip to hold onto her full, round ass cheek. Pulling her tightly against him, he whispered into her ear, "I meant what I said about fucking you three times before dinner. I think the first time I'm going to take you while we're both still mostly dressed."

Her hand touched his cheek and he moved to look into her deep, nearly black eyes. She whispered, "Love me any way you want, Sean. I know without a doubt it'll be fantastic."

Lauren's words simultaneously squeezed his heart as they made his cock turn rock hard. She had such trust in him.

After giving her a gentle kiss, he nuzzled her cheek and whispered, "You are all the Christmas present I need. I love you."

His human tightened her grip on his arms and whispered, "I love you, too. But I do want one more present from you."

Moving back to look into her eyes, he said, "Right now you're thinking of presents?"

She gave a sexy smile and he knew she was up to something. "What I want won't kill you."

Kneading her ass cheek, he whispered, "Then tell me because my restraint is about to snap in that way you like so much."

"That's what I want, Sean. You, unrestrained and inside me. I want to be able to feel how hard you fucked me for the rest of the night."

CHAPTER TWO

Six months ago, Lauren never would've had the nerve to ask any man to fuck her, let alone in a husky whisper, but Sean had changed all of that. The cougar-shifter treated sex as being necessary to happiness and nothing to be ashamed of. She tended to agree with him.

Before she could think of anything else, Sean squeezed her ass and lowered his head. A hairbreadth away from her lips, his words were a hot caress as he said, "As you wish, baby," before taking her lips in a possessive kiss.

Opening at once, his tongue slipped inside her mouth and she threaded her fingers through his hair. She met him stroke for stroke, and tilted her head to have better access to his mouth.

Damn, his heat, his taste, and even his scent made her even wetter.

Sean growled and backed them up against a wall, not hard enough to hurt her, but enough to let her know his cougar-side was coming out to play.

One hand moved between them to pinch her nipple and Lauren cried out. Sean pinched again before running his hand down her ribs, her stomach, only to stop just shy of her clit. Wiggling, she tried to tell him she wanted to feel his fingers through the shimmery material of her baby doll lingerie, but instead of touching her, he removed his hand.

Growling in frustration, she was about to break the kiss to ask what the hell he was doing when she felt his hard, hot cock where his hand had just been.

When had he done that?

She moved one of her hands down his back to land on his tight, round ass only to feel the fabric of his jeans under her fingers.

He really was going to fuck her with his clothes on, and she found it hot.

Sean broke the kiss at the same time he rubbed the head of his cock against her clit, the friction of the material making her legs weak. Only because she clung to his neck with one hand did she remain standing.

Sean's voice was husky when he said, "Are you wet and aching for me?"

He gave an extra swirl on her clit and she hissed, "Yes."

"Good."

Her cougar-shifter moved his arm behind her to under her ass and lifted. Before she could wrap her legs around his waist, he thrust his hard, long cock into her with one swift motion.

Gripping his neck harder, she reveled in how deliciously his cock filled her up. "Mm, yes."

After his eyes flashed cougar blue, he grabbed the back of her head with his free hand and pulled her down for a kiss as he moved, his cock stroking hard and deep into her pussy. Her already sensitive nipples grew more so as the lace of her lingerie rubbed against them; the silky material on the lower half of her body felt like a cool whisper against her skin.

Tightening his grip around her ass, Sean pounded harder, the sound of the flesh slapping against flesh all but drowning out everything else.

At least, until Sean growled into her mouth. The vibrations sent a tingle through her body, straight to her clit. Even without his fingers touching between her legs, she was close. So close.

A few more hard thrusts and she broke the kiss to cry out as pleasure shot through her body. She held on for dear life as her cougar-shifter continued to move in and out as she spasmed around his cock. Just as she came down from her orgasm, Sean growled with one last thrust before he held her close and bit where her neck met her shoulder. The delicate sting caused by his elongated feline fangs sent her over the edge again.

She'd barely formed a coherent thought before her man whispered into her ear, "This time, I'm going to lick every inch of your body before I allow you to come."

Shivering, Lauren knew he was telling the truth. He was about to torture her in the best possible way, and she would never get enough.

~ ~ ~

An hour later, Sean lay on the couch with Lauren sprawled on top of him, his human female stroking his chest with her soft, delicate fingers. Even after all this time, he sometimes worried that his animal side would be too much for her; shifters were fond of sex that was hard and rough. But after the first few times they'd been together, she'd opened up to him to the point that one day soon she'd be able to outlast him. Hell, she'd soon be as demanding as any shifter female.

Without thinking, he chuckled and Lauren looked up at him. "What's so funny?"

Hugging his completely naked human tighter, he said, "I was just comparing the first time we had sex to just now."

22

She frowned. "Be careful, Fisher. Christmas Eve or not, I can still leave your ass cold and alone tonight."

He reached a hand up and brushed her cheek with his knuckles. "Always the threats before I have a chance to speak." Her frown deepened and he grinned. "But I love your mouth, so don't ever change."

Her lips twitched as she battled a smile. "Well, let's just say I'm practice for meeting my family. My older brother is as stubborn as any of the shifters I've met thus far. He's nearly as tall, too."

"You sure there's no secret shifter blood in the Spencer family tree?"

As she shook her head, her long, straightened, black hair tickled his chest. "I don't think so. The Spencers are just stubborn. And maybe a bit argumentative."

"A bit?"

She gave a playful slap against his chest. "Look who's talking, buddy. You need me to keep you in check. Who the hell knows what would happen if you were let loose on your own."

The words were meant to be teasing, but all of the sudden, all Sean could think about was how he wanted Lauren with him.

Always.

His inner cougar chirped. *Yes. Ask her. Now. Make a claim. She is ready.*

Lauren must've notice his lack of response because she laid a hand on his cheek and said, "What are you thinking, Sean? I see your heart in your eyes."

Six months ago, Sean would've balked at showing his true feelings so plainly on his face, but with Lauren, he never had to hide who or what he was. She accepted him.

They may be naked under the flashing Christmas lights, but it was time.

He cupped her cheek and his voice was low when he said, "I want you as my mate."

His human blinked and whispered, "What?"

Sean wasn't about to back down. "Mated, married, we can do it both ways, but I want to spend the rest of my life with you." Emotion choked his throat at the thought of her saying no. He couldn't lose her. "I can wait, baby. It just felt right to ask."

Giving a wobbly smile, Lauren slapped his chest again. "I don't want to wait, Sean Fisher, but you know it's against the law."

Rubbing his thumb against her soft cheek, he whispered, "Marriage might be, but we could be mated by my clan, and make it official the human way as soon as it's legal. Momentum is building to make that happen."

As she silently stared into his eyes, his heart rate kicked up. Maybe he'd asked too soon. Or, maybe she didn't love him as much as he'd thought. After all, they would face censure just about everywhere they went until the laws changed and human-shifter pairings became more common.

Afraid this might be the last time he held her, he hugged her close. If she said no, Sean wasn't sure he'd be able to just let her go. Human or not, Lauren Spencer was worth fighting for.

She opened her mouth and he held his breath. "Oh, Sean, I would love to be your mate, but how would it work? We can't live together, we can't be married, and we'd always be looking over our shoulders for a cop. Is that what you want?"

She didn't say no. Grabbing on to that small piece of hope, he said, "We could make it work."

"How, Sean? I need specifics before I get my hopes up."

"Well, you're nearly done with your dental training. Have you ever considered becoming a shifter-specialized dentist? You

24

could set up a practice on DarkStalker's land. I'm sure my clan would love to have you."

She searched his eyes. "Are you asking me to move in with your clan? Do they know about this?"

He moved his hand from her cheek to the back of her neck and squeezed. "I haven't asked. I wanted to ask you first."

~~~

Her heart thumping in her ears, Lauren couldn't believe Sean had asked her to be his mate. The thought of never having this shifter male tease her, touch her, or hold her close made her heart squeeze. She hadn't known where their relationship was going, as the law forbade human-shifter marriages, but now all she could think about was spending the rest of her life with Sean Fisher.

Yet Lauren was far too logical to say yes without thinking things through. After all, it wasn't just her life that would be turned upside down if she said yes; her family, and his, would have to accept them as well.

He squeezed the back of her neck again and Lauren realized she hadn't responded. Laying a hand on his jaw, she said, "Maybe."

He blinked. "Maybe?"

"Yes, maybe. First, I want you to meet my parents and charm them like no tomorrow. Then, we can go to your clan. I want to meet them before I even start thinking about living amongst a pack of cougar-shifters."

One corner of his mouth ticked up. "At least we're not wolves."

"Sean."

"Okay, okay, I'll be serious."

She raised an eyebrow. "So when am I meeting your clan?"

He chuckled. "Funny you should ask as I spoke to my sister earlier today about that. She's determined to scare you off."

"Oh, is she? Well, maybe I should buy her a scratching post for Christmas and throw down my challenge."

Caressing the back of her neck, he leaned up and placed a kiss on her lips. "Have I mentioned recently that I love you?"

"Maybe." She kissed his jaw and then his ear before she whispered, "But I think you should show me how much, just to try to sway my decision into the yes column."

He slapped her ass. "You know you'd miss my 'surprises' if you left me."

Sean had a tendency of showing up in random places and convincing her to have sex in bathrooms, parks, hell, he'd even made her come with his fingers one night while they'd been out to dinner at a shifter-run restaurant. "Yes, but who would miss having a woman around who allows those kinds of surprises?"

"Allows? Baby, one touch and you melt in my hands."

"Then make me melt again, Sean Fisher, and my Christmas Eve will be complete."

As he kissed her and hugged her tightly against him, she pushed any worry she had about their families to the back burner. If worse came to worst, and neither his clan nor her family could accept the mating, this might be the last night she had with her cougar and she would make it count.

CHAPTER THREE

The next morning, they were driving in silence when *that* song came on the radio. Sean groaned just as Lauren squealed and jacked up the volume to the rock version of Carol of the Bells.

As she waved her hands in the air in time to the beat, his inner cougar growled. Not that Sean could blame him; the first time he'd heard the song, it'd been cool. But after two hundred times in the span of a week, he was ready to rip the stereo out of the car and forgo any music at all if it meant he wouldn't have to hear the song ever again.

Glancing over, some of his irritation eased as Lauren swayed to the music. Maybe this song wouldn't be so bad if his female swayed to it while she was naked.

Yes, if she were naked and swaying, she could listen to the same song a thousand times, and he wouldn't care.

Tearing his eyes away, he focused back on the road. Despite being the busiest freeway in the state, I-5 was dead this early in the morning on Christmas Day. Lauren had wanted to spend the entire day with her family, so they could get to know him, and right now, he needed as many bonus points as he could until she agreed to be his mate.

Especially since meeting his clan would be ten times worse for his human than him meeting her family. DarkStalker was cautious, and while they'd recently accepted one of their own mating a wolf-shifter, mating a human was a whole different ballgame since it was illegal.

But it wasn't as if he would put his clan at any serious risk. DarkStalker's clan leader, Kian Murray, was one of the smartest men he'd ever met, and if there was ever a shifter to find a legal loophole allowing Sean to mate a human, it would be Kian. Provided the Spencer family accepted him, first thing tomorrow he'd call his leader and ask for his advice.

As the song ended, Lauren turned down the music, but before he could tease her about her weird obsession, something smacked into his bumper. The car spun and his reflexes kicked in. He tried to keep his steering wheel straight, but something slammed into him again, knocking his grip loose. The wheel spun out of control, and his last thought was of Lauren before the car crashed headfirst into the roadside barrier and the world went black.

~~~

Lauren opened her eyes to find a white, inflated airbag in front of her face. Blinking a few times, the fog lifted from her brain at the same time pain radiated up her left leg. She groaned, and then remembered Sean. "Sean? Babe? Are you okay?"

When there was nothing but silence, a bad feeling gathered in the pit of her stomach. He'd better be alive, damn it. He couldn't leave her like this.

She pushed against the airbag until it deflated. Turning to the side, she found the driver's seat empty. The door was open, so she yelled, "Sean!"

The answering silence made her heart skip a beat. Her shifter would never abandon her. Lauren needed to get out of the car and see if he'd been thrown to the side.

Oh, god. What if he'd been thrown and broken his neck? Shifters healed fast, but not even her cougar-shifter could survive that.

Breathing in and out, she forced her panic down. Freaking out about "what ifs" would accomplish nothing, so she fell back on her usual logical self and determined the first step was getting free of the car.

A quick check told her that apart from her leg, the rest of her injuries appeared to be superficial. They'd been lucky to hit whatever it was head on rather than on her side or she might be dead.

Moving the deflated airbag out of the way, it took a few tries until she could undo her seatbelt and open the door. She leaned her head out and peeked, but she didn't spot any people or other cars, except for the occasional person driving past. Rather than wonder why no one would stop to check on them, Lauren eased out of the car and noticed the long gash on her left leg. It wasn't gushing out blood, which was good, but it hurt like hell so she still kept most of her weight on her good leg as she pushed herself up.

Once upright, her head spun for a second, but she gritted her teeth and remained standing. She needed to see if Sean was okay.

Favoring her right leg, she limped around the back of the car until she could see the driver's side, but her shifter was nowhere to be found. The small pool of blood right outside his car door made her stomach churn as she realized this might not have been an accident after all.

"Shit." She should have told Sean about that car following her last night. Some small part of her brain screamed that the two were related.

If this were a normal situation, she'd wait for the state patrol to show up, report what had happened, and ask for their help. But Lauren was a human and Sean was a shifter, which meant talking to the state troopers or the police might land her in jail.

Think, Lauren, think. She wasn't about to abandon the love of her life, but who would help her?

Then it hit her—his clan. If she could find a way to contact them, they should listen to her long enough to gather the facts. They might toss her aside after that, but none of that mattered as long as she secured the help Sean needed.

There was only a matter of minutes before a passerby stopped or the state troopers showed up, so Lauren limped to the driver's seat and confronted more blood. Normally, she wasn't squeamish at the sight of blood; she saw it often enough when working on her dental patients. But this wasn't just any blood; it was her boyfriend's blood.

Stop it. Focus, or who will help him? With a deep inhalation, she leaned down and looked for Sean's phone. He always tossed it into one of the drink holder slots under the stereo console, but both of them were empty. Clenching her jaw, she sat down on the blood-covered seat and fished around his seat, and still came up with nothing. She turned, and after feeling around the floor of the backseat, her hand came into contact with a hard, rectangular object. *Bingo.*

After checking that the phone still worked, she grabbed her purse from under the passenger side seat, maneuvered herself upright again, and limped for the grass on the side of the road. There were some trees not too far away, but with the pain in her leg, it took three times as long to reach them. Just in time too, as the sirens blared in the distance.

Once she was far enough inside the trees to be hidden from view, Lauren took another fortifying breath. She hoped Sean had told his clan leader about their relationship because she was about to call him.

She looked through Sean's phone until she found the name Kian Murray. She may never have visited Clan DarkStalker, but Sean had told her a little about their clan leader. While DarkStalker's leader didn't hate humans outright, he could still blame her for Sean's disappearance and leave her to the human police.

No, she needed to stop with all the guilt about not telling Sean about the tail last night. She and Sean had been careful, but whenever people had discovered her boyfriend was a shifter, they'd suffered their fair share of jeering and threats. The person who had hit them could be any one of those people. After all, she had no proof it was Human Purity or any of the extremist "humans only" groups.

With her guilt pushed back for now, she hit the call button and the phone rang once before a male voice answered, "Hello?"

Her heart was pounding as she answered, "Is this Kian Murray?"

"You're not Sean. Who is this?"

He was trying to intimidate her with his tone, but she wasn't having it. "This is Lauren Spencer, Sean's fiancée. He's been taken, and I need your help."

~~~

Pain throbbing at the back of his head was the first thing Sean noticed when he regained consciousness. The pounding made it hard to concentrate, but then he remembered the accident; he needed to wake the hell up and get Lauren to safety. Whoever had hit his car had done it on purpose and who knew what they'd do to his female.

He gritted his teeth against the pain, and with incredible effort, Sean opened his eyes to find himself in a dim-lit room.

Fuck. This wasn't a hospital, or even the makeshift clinic on DarkStalker's lands. His cougar eyesight was keen even in the dark, and the room was no more than fifteen feet by twenty feet. No tables, beds, sofas, or anything else apart from the chair under his ass and one tall, metal cabinet across the room.

And most important of all, there was no Lauren.

Where the hell is she? He needed to find his female. If whoever hit his car had hurt her, they would pay.

His cougar snarled in agreement. *Yes. She is ours. We must find her.*

In order to do that, he needed to find a way out. He tried to move his hands, but pain shot up his arms at the same time his wrists and hands came up against some kind of bindings.

Drawing in a hiss, Sean realized he was trapped. His fingers were folded into his palm with his thumb on top, and wrapped with some kind of super strong bindings, which had been placed to prevent him from not only using his claws, but also from shifting. If he shifted in this position, his arms would break in cougar-form. His chances of getting away would be nearly zero after that. He'd have to come up with another strategy.

The lock on the door clicked. With every bit of stubbornness he possessed, Sean pushed his pain to the back of his mind so he could focus. He might be one of his clan's engineers, but all of DarkStalker's clan members received training as teenagers on how to defend and escape. There were always humans who wanted to harm them, and one of the few things all shifter clans agreed upon was that their members needed to be ready in case of an attack.

The door opened to reveal a man and woman wearing jeans and sweaters, but also with cloth bandit-style black masks over their faces. That signaled the pair were with Human Purity. Despite how loud the fuckers were with their protests and outrage, they hid behind scraps of material to avoid being targeted and hunted down.

Shifters might be civil ninety-five percent of the time, but Human Purity feared that remaining five percent, and with good reason. If this pair had killed his female, he would make the bastards pay.

The human male approached him, his head high and shoulders back. The bindings around his hands must be pretty fucking special to instill this kind of confidence in the human.

The male stopped two feet away from Sean. When he spoke, his voice was loud and his tone rushed, as if the man came from the east coast. "A trial was held with the board, and you've been found guilty of intent to dilute the human gene pool. Once we confirm the woman you've corrupted is clean and free of any shifter hybrid offspring, she will be rehabilitated. Then you will receive your sentence."

He tried to clench his hands, but the bindings prevented it. While it was highly unlikely Lauren was pregnant since she was on birth control, if she was and these bastards took their baby without her consent, he would find their weakness and exploit it to cause pain. They needed to experience the same sense of loss as he and his female would if they killed their baby.

First things first, he needed more information.

Despite his inner anger, Sean kept his face impassive. He needed to make Lauren appear to mean nothing to him. "The human female was fun, but nothing serious. Do what you will with her. I want to know what the hell you intend to do with me."

Because of the black masks, he couldn't read the facial expressions of either of the Human Purity members. That pissed him off big time since he had no idea if they bought his words or not. He'd have to rely on his supersensitive hearing and sense of smell to gauge their reactions.

And right now, he didn't scent fear or hear any racing heartbeats. These two were very confident.

This time, the human female spoke, her voice holding a southern drawl. "You will be made an example to discourage shifters and humans from mixing. That is all you need to know."

It was time to try to wheedle information out of the pair. "Then why bother coming in here to tell me anything? You could've done it over an intercom system."

Rather than answer, the female lifted up a video camera and held it out in front of her. Once she nodded, the male approached him and Sean had a feeling he knew what was coming. Human Purity used videos to recruit new members; kicking the shit out of a shifter always worked well for them.

The male moved behind him and every muscle in Sean's body tensed. As the seconds ticked by, he didn't allow the silence to unsettle him. The best thing right now, for both him and Lauren, was to brace himself for whatever blow was coming. If Purity's past videos were anything to go on, they wouldn't kill him straight away; they liked to make the shifters suffer for days.

That meant Sean needed to remain conscious and with the least amount of injuries possible so he could think of a plan.

Without warning, a punch landed on his side, but Sean was careful not to make a sound. Acting stoic may hurt him in the long run, but it would fuel Purity's hatred to keep him alive longer to suffer more.

Or so he hoped. He needed more time to get out of this situation. Lauren was in trouble because of him, and he needed to make it right.

Another punch landed on his opposite side and Sean concentrated. This session might go from painful to what-the-fuckery fast, and he needed to be ready.

Chapter Four

Lauren hugged her body tighter. Despite her winter coat, the cold had seeped all the way to the bone. Sitting outside, wedged between two huge boulders, while sitting on a wet rock in December, would do that to a person.

If Sean were there, he would've wrapped his arms around her and let his extra warm shifter body heat chase the chill away. But Sean was gone. She refused to think he was dead, which was why she sat here in the cold, waiting for one of his clan members to come get her.

Kian Murray hadn't said much. She'd recounted the events leading up to the car crash, and then described her location. He'd given her instructions about where she could wait nearby in safety, until one of his clan, wearing a stretchy red band around his or her neck, retrieved her.

She hadn't had a chance to ask who before the shifter leader had hung up. Yes, she knew he had to be careful and exude strength in order to protect his clan, but he'd been almost rude with her. Whether that was because she was human or because she'd referred to herself as Sean's fiancée, she didn't know.

Rubbing her arms with her hands for warmth, Lauren gave a sad smile. She'd never officially said yes, but if the trauma and possibility of Sean being dead had taught her anything, it was that she wanted to keep Sean. Forever.

COUGAR'S FIRST CHRISTMAS

Even if it meant living with the shifters and becoming a shifter dentist. When—not if—she saw him, she'd tell him yes, she wanted to be his mate. Of course, if he still wanted her after she shared her other Christmas present-slash-secret with him.

An engine roared past and Lauren held her breath. Each and every car that came close to the road scared her into thinking the human state troopers would find her and take her away. She wanted to trust Kian Murray, but couldn't. For all she knew, he had sent a human police officer to retrieve her and take her away. Then she would no longer be his problem.

Get a grip, Lauren. As she was injured, alone, and on Human Purity's shit list, she really didn't have a choice but to believe Kian would help her.

She extended her good leg and lowered it, hoping to warm her body up with some exercise, when a blue-eyed cougar appeared in front of her. For a second, her heart skipped a beat at the huge feline in front of her, but then she realized there were no wild cougars in this small, forested area since it was nestled between two cities. The cat had to be a shifter.

With her fear mostly pushed aside, Lauren studied the cougar looking at her. He or she was smaller than Sean, with more spots on his or her nose. Yet the blue color of its eyes were identical to her man when he was in his cat form. She'd never seen another shifter in their animal form apart from Sean, but she wondered if the same eye color signaled a relation.

The cougar was also wearing a red band around its throat.

Before she could speak, the cougar butted her knee and then motioned with its head to the side. Lauren whispered, "Are you with DarkStalker?"

The big cat gave a soft meow and turned around, swishing its tail. Again, it made a motion with its head before taking another step away.

Lauren wanted to follow, but she needed at least one more confirmation. She whispered again, "Wait." The cat looked over its shoulder and she continued, "Prove to me that you're friendly and with DarkStalker. Come here and let me touch the top of your head."

The cat flicked its tail and gave a low growl, as if saying no fucking way.

Yet Lauren wasn't about to trust so easily. Crossing her arms over her chest, she raised an eyebrow and waited. After about a minute, the cat gave a soft growl and padded over to her. When Lauren didn't reach out right away, the cougar tilted its head as if asking for her to hurry up.

Since the big cat would've attacked her already if he or she had intended it, Lauren reached out a hand and lightly scratched the top of the cougar's head. The tanned fur under her finger tips wasn't as soft as a domestic cat's, but it wasn't too rough. After a few scratches the cougar turned around again and motioned with its head.

Satisfied for now, she placed her hands on the boulders to either side of her and used the strength of her arms to maneuver herself upright. The cougar's eyes shot straight to her injured leg. Lauren said, "Don't worry. It stopped bleeding and isn't too bad. Once I get somewhere warm, I'll be fine."

The cat studied her a second before nodding and walking away.

Lauren limped behind through some thick underbrush before the cat stopped and looked at her. Hoping for some clarification, Lauren said, "Where do we go from here?"

The cougar chirped and then she watched as the cat's face morphed into a human's head, her legs extended into human legs, and her paws turned into hands. A tall, red-haired, and very naked woman wearing a stretchy red band around her throat stood in front of her. The shifter female crossed her arms over her chest before giving Lauren a once over and saying, "So this is my brother's female."

Lauren blinked. While the woman and Sean shared the same shape of eyes and light blue eye color, that's where the resemblance ended; Sean had brown hair to this woman's red. "You're Sean's sister?"

"Glad to see my brother couldn't be bothered to show you a picture of his beloved older sister." The woman reached over and retrieved something from the tree next to her. As the shifter tore off the red band and tossed the sweatshirt over her head, she said, "Yes, I'm Danika. Since he talks about you all the time, I know you're Lauren Spencer."

Lauren's momentary shock faded and she remembered why she'd contacted DarkStalker in the first place. "Have you found Sean yet? Or, at least, have an idea of where he is?"

Danika tugged on a pair of sweatpants and then looked her dead in the eye. "No, not yet, but my clan is working on it."

Her throat tightened, but she fought the urge to cry. "Do you think he's still alive?"

Irritation flashed through the shifter's eyes. "Yes. If you're willing to give up on him so easily, then you don't deserve him."

Lauren narrowed her eyes. "Of course I haven't given up. Do you think I would have waited out here in the freezing cold for over an hour for you to find me? I stayed because I can't find him alone. Maybe I know something that can help."

"Yes, my leader seems to think so too."

Any lasting shock from the woman's shifting from cat to human faded at Danika's tone and was replaced with irritation and a little bit of anger. "Just spit out whatever you're not saying. Sean does the same thing when he's frustrated or angry, and I never allow him to stew, so I won't put up with it from you either. I thought shifters were above passive-aggression."

Danika raised an eyebrow. "Well, well, the human is tougher than she looks."

"I wouldn't have a shifter for a fiancée if I weren't."

After a second, Sean's sister nodded. "So far, I like you."

Standing up to the shifter female seemed to be working, so Lauren kept at it. "Well if you do, then can we get going? My leg hurts like hell, my toes on my good leg are starting to go numb, and I'm wearing blood-soaked clothes."

"Fine, follow me. I'll take you to one of DarkStalker's apartments in the area to get cleaned up. Then we'll see if you're any use to us."

Once the shifter turned her back, Lauren let out a long breath as she followed Danika through the woods. If it took this much energy to handle one shifter, what would it be like to face a whole room of them, let alone an entire clan?

Think of Sean. You love him. You can do this.

For Sean, she'd do anything. She just hoped she could change her clothes and eat something before she had to try to win over any more stubborn shifters.

~~~

Looking in the bathroom mirror, Lauren made a face and decided there was nothing she could do about the curly frizzy mess that was her hair. The apartment Danika had brought her to lacked any of the hair care products she usually used to straighten it.

Of course, worrying about her hair was just the latest excuse she was using to stay inside the bathroom. By now,

Danika's friends should've shown up, which meant dealing with more shifters and trying to gain more acceptance.

She wouldn't mind all of this if Sean was at her side. But alone, it was going to be downright exhausting.

At least her leg felt better after the hot shower and a liberal application of antiseptic gel. She'd been right in her earlier assumption that while long, the cut wasn't deep.

Stop dillydallying and coming up with excuses, Lauren. Think of Sean. With one last glance at her reflection in the mirror, she turned and opened the door. As she walked down the hallway, she heard a male's voice say, "According to Dave, Human Purity doesn't try to hide their tracks. He should have a list of possible locations to search in the next hour or two."

Danika's voice greeted her ears next. "I don't like waiting, but knowing Sean, he'll find a way to keep them from killing him in the next two hours. I'm more concerned about having enough shifters we trust to investigate the list of locations."

There was a pause and then the male voice said, "Hello, human. Care to come out and join the conversation? I promise I won't bite."

The male shifter's light tone eased a bit of her nervousness. Maybe not all shifters were as hardass as Danika Fisher.

Straightening her shoulders, Lauren strode into the living room and was greeted with the sight of a muscled man with amusement dancing in his green eyes. He was tall, as all shifters tended to be, but since he wasn't glaring at her the way Danika had back in the forest, he was a little less intimidating.

The male smiled. "So this is Sean's human? If I weren't mated myself, I'd be tempted to try to woo you."

She battled a flush. Human men had rarely noticed her over the years, but she attracted shifters like a fly with honey. "And you are?"

The male strode over and held out a hand. "I'm Sylas Murray of Clan GreyFire."

It took her a second to recognize the name. "The wolf-shifter clan?"

He winked. "The very one. My mate is GreyFire's clan leader, Kaya."

He wiggled his fingers, and Lauren took his hand to shake. Once she finished and dropped it, she looked over to Danika and then back to Sylas. "I don't understand. Sean is a cougar-shifter. From what little I know, the wolves and cougars don't much care for each other."

Danika's tone was dry when she said, "It's taken me months to get use to the stench of wolf, but despite their smell, they have their uses."

Sylas shook his head. "What Dani is trying to say is that I'm a cougar-shifter too, but I'm mated to a wolf. My brother, Kian, is DarkStalker's clan leader, so I have ties to both clans. You could say I'm the reason the two clans are now getting along."

Danika rolled her eyes. "Yes, you and not the virus we helped with."

Sylas shrugged. "Hey, the virus helped, but you know it's all down to me and my sexy talk. Kaya didn't stand a chance."

As the two continued to banter, Lauren tried to take it all in, but was having trouble. A few months ago, Sean had started to trust her with his clan's affairs, but she was still human, and there was so much she didn't know.

Watching the pair argue like brother and sister, Lauren decided she needed to stop them so she could get answers and bring their focus back on Sean.

Sean. He needed their help, and she would remind them of that fact.

COUGAR'S FIRST CHRISTMAS

Lauren gave a loud whistle and the two shifters stopped talking to stare at her. Fueled by her love for Sean, she said, "Enough. Right now, I don't care how or why you're working together. All I want to know is what is being done to find Sean. I overheard that you're tracking the location, but unsure about having enough bodies to help. What can we do to fix that?"

Dani frowned, but Sy grinned before he said, "Yes, I think I like you, human."

Danika gave Sylas a shove before she answered, "Your drive to save Sean raises you in my esteem, but there isn't much for you to do but wait around. You're a dentist, not a soldier."

She opened her mouth to protest, but Sylas cut her off. "As much as I hate to say it, she's right. But hang tight. If Sean's in a bad way when we find him, we'll need your help. That's why my brother wanted Dani to bring you here to wait."

As much as she didn't want to think of Sean in a "bad way," Lauren would rather be prepared. "What? How?"

Danika explained, "Shifters usually have control of their inner animals, but sometimes, when they've been severely injured or feel threatened, the animal side takes over. When that happens, it's about a fifty-fifty chance of bringing the human side back."

She tried to imagine Sean wild with an animal-frenzy, but couldn't picture it. She'd known her boyfriend was a cougar-shifter, but he'd never, not once, given her a reason to fear his animal side. "Only fifty-fifty?"

Sylas added, "That's where you come in. When someone both the human and animal sides love tries to coax them back from the brink, be it family or a mate, the odds of saving them increases exponentially. The only real question is, are you confident in your love for Sean and his for you? Because if you're not, Sean may kill you in that state."

Without missing a beat, Lauren nodded. "Of course. I love Sean Fisher. He's my best friend, and I'd rather die than live without him."

Sylas nodded in approval. "Good. Let's hope it doesn't come to that, but I feel better with you being prepared." The male shifter glanced at Danika. "Feed her, Dani, while I tap my contacts."

"No, Sy, you feed her. I have a far bigger reach than you, and you know it."

Lauren interjected, "Why don't you both try to reach people? As long as there's food in the kitchen, I can feed myself. I'm a big girl."

One side of Sy's mouth ticked up. "Good human. The fridge is stocked, so have at it."

She was about to turn around and head for the kitchen when Danika said, "Oh, and a doctor is coming to check you out properly. So eat fast."

At the word "doctor," Lauren prevented herself from showing any emotion on her face. While she wanted to make sure she was all right, she was afraid the doctor might discover her secret and then deliver the bad news.

She kept a steady face and nodded.

Her mask must've been convincing because no sooner had she given her confirmation, Danika looked back over to Sylas and began discussing who to call.

Well, at least that discussion had been avoided. If anyone deserved to hear about her secret first, it was Sean.

Lauren limped to the kitchen and hoped these shifters knew what they were doing. The longer Sean was missing, the greater her fear grew concerning Sean making it out of this alive.

Hold on, babe. You haven't given me a chance to say yes.

44

COUGAR'S FIRST CHRISTMAS

In that moment, Lauren realized the best Christmas gift she could ever hope for was to have Sean alive and back in her arms again.

CHAPTER FIVE

Sean was finally alone again. The male human bastard had throttled him for nearly half an hour before he stopped to give an overly enthusiastic speech into the video camera.

The speech hadn't told him much apart from "a large-scale attack was coming soon." They'd only let him hear that, and the call for more recruits to reply to the video for more information, because they assumed he'd be dead soon.

Sean hoped to disappoint them on that front.

He scanned the room around him more slowly than before, now that he was alone, to try to find something to help him escape.

He didn't see any two-way mirrors for observation or anything that looked like a camera. Human Purity wasn't completely stupid; the less evidence they had of his kidnapping, the less chance of a conviction. Even with the video of the male punching him, they'd be careful to block out both their faces.

Not like the US Shifter Department of Justice would take much notice. They were understaffed and overworked. A single kidnapping was low on their list of priorities.

The reminder that he was on his own, at least until his clan knew he was missing, focused Sean. He might be the only one who could save Lauren. He needed to find a way out of here.

But no matter how much he studied the room, he didn't see anything that would cut through his bindings.

Ignoring the pain from his injured shoulder, he tried pulling his hands apart again, but nothing. The material wouldn't budge.

He then closed his eyes and focused on the position of his fingers. As he wiggled them the minuscule amount allowed by his bindings, he realized something about the fourth finger on both of his hands. If he extended his claw and pierced through his palm, he might just be able to cut through the material on the other side.

Sure, it would hurt like hell, but given the amount of pain he already was in from the car accident and his beating, a little more was no big deal. Especially if it meant he could be free to find Lauren and make sure she was all right.

Concentrating, Sean extended the claw on his ring finger of his right hand and clenched his jaw as the sharp point poked through his palm. He felt it pierce the other side and into the binding material. Gearing himself up for more pain, Sean then moved his claw up and down through his palm. The bones of his fingers made it difficult to move more than a little, but it was enough. He could feel the claw catch on the bindings. He'd have to do both sides, and then he might just be able to pull his hands apart.

Since the blood from his wounds would drip onto the floor and alert anyone from Human Purity who came to check on him, he focused on his task. He had one shot at freedom, and the next time the door opened on the far side of the room, he'd be ready to spring. Given the confidence of the pair he'd seen earlier, combined with the normal-looking lock on the door, his prison probably wasn't that secure. One shifter against a handful of humans were good enough odds that even with his injuries, he might be able to escape.

Gritting his teeth against the pain, he continued slicing through the binding material. *Hold on, Lauren. I'm coming.*

Rescuing her was his top priority. It helped him to forget that after this, Lauren might want nothing to do with him.

No. He would fight for her. He loved his human, and he would protect her. No more hiding from his clan; he would introduce Lauren and ensure she had the protection of Clan DarkStalker for the rest of her life whether she wanted it or not.

~~~

Lauren blinked at the blonde-haired, green-eyed woman who called herself "Dr. Lisa." Although she hadn't said as much, judging by her height and familiarity with Sylas Murray, Lauren suspected the woman was a shifter.

The doctor was poking and prodding her abdomen as she said, "Does it hurt here?"

"No."

Lisa removed her hands and stood up. "While scans would give me a better answer, my preliminary exam didn't find anything life threatening."

"So I can help with Sean, if they need me?"

"I don't like it, but it's not like I can stop you."

The doctor remained quiet and Lauren realized if this woman were a shifter, she could finally get the answers she's been looking for. She blurted out, "Are you a shifter?"

"Yes. I assumed Sy or Dani would've told you that." She gave a long look and then continued, "Since you claim to be a shifter's fiancée, I'm guessing it doesn't bother you that a shifter just touched your skin. So tell me why you burned to ask me that question."

The female shifter was very calm, collected, and logical. That made Lauren like her all the more than the flirty Sylas or gruff Danika.

Especially since Lauren had some questions she'd itched to ask for months now, but hadn't known whom to ask. Of course, two weeks ago, the need to find answers had become more pressing. She wasn't about to pass up this chance. "I want to ask you some biology questions, but if I do, will it qualify as doctor-patient confidentiality?"

"As long as it doesn't endanger any of the shifter clans in the Cascade Mountains, then yes, ask away."

Lauren picked at her borrowed sweatpants, suddenly nervous. But no, she needed an answer to prepare herself before talking with Sean. So she asked, "Do babies conceived between humans and shifters turn out okay?"

The shifter doctor stared at her a second before she asked, "How far along are you?"

That answer made her heart sink. "Why? Will it not survive to full-term? Please just tell me, Doctor. I need to know."

"Because of the laws, it's rare for shifters and humans to conceive, but it has been done many times before. Just like with any pregnancy, there are risks, but there is no reason your child shouldn't survive and be born healthy."

A huge weight suddenly lifted from Lauren's shoulders. At first, when she'd taken the pregnancy test last week to try to confirm her suspicions, the test had resulted in a half-plus symbol, which was neither positive nor negative. Four more tests all turned out the same way, making her think humans and shifters weren't supposed to have children.

But now, if what Dr. Lisa said was true, her baby might live.

Dr. Lisa's green eyes were stern yet inquisitive. Lauren decided to give her more details. "I missed my period about two and a half weeks ago. Combined with fatigue and lack of appetite, I suspected I might be pregnant. I stopped taking my birth control pills just in case. The tests I took all came out weird, so I wasn't sure what to think."

"And you couldn't go to a human hospital for fear of arrest or a forced abortion."

"Yes."

"I'm going to hazard a guess that you didn't tell Sean, let alone Sy and Dani about this." Lauren shook her head and the doctor let out a sigh. "I really wish you would have. If Sean knew his female was carrying his child, he would've taken better security measures to ensure your safety."

Lauren knew the shifters had their own way of doing things, but if she didn't set a line now about her opinions, it might be too late. Straightening her shoulders, Lauren said, "There will always be risks and I'd rather face them than be kept in a glass cage."

The doctor smiled. "I feel about the same way, although be prepared, Lauren. Sean will turn into a possessive, protective male once he knows the truth. As difficult as it may be to do it, allow him to be a little more protective of you. Otherwise, he may turn wild."

"Why does everyone keep mentioning Sean turning wild? He's never been that way with me, not even in the worst of our fights."

"That's a good sign. But just prepare yourself, because shifter men aren't human; denying their animal sides will eat away at them until they turn into an unhappy, depressed mess."

"An unhappy, depressed mess? Is that your clinical explanation?"

Lisa snorted. "A more apt description is a fucking mess, but I was trying to be somewhat polite."

Lauren smiled. "I like a doctor who's honest." Sobering back up again, she continued, "Will you be my doctor?"

"I'm a GreyFire wolf-shifter, but if Kian will allow me to visit once you move to DarkStalker's land, then I would be delighted. It would give us more information about human-shifter pregnancies that could end up saving lives in the future."

She didn't like the idea of being a test subject, but she'd put up with it if it meant she could have Dr. Lisa.

There was a knock on the door and Dr. Lisa said, "Come in. The exam's over."

Sy opened the door and poked his head in. "We've narrowed it down to two locations in the area. Is Lauren cleared to go? I need both of you to come with me. We might need you."

The doctor nodded. "As long as you don't bring her into the den of snakes, then yes, she can go."

The two women shared a look and Lauren nodded in understanding; she needed to be careful of the baby, especially after the recent car accident.

Lauren turned toward Sylas. "So, where are we going?"

~~~

Both of Sean's palms throbbed as he waited for his next visitor. It had taken at least an hour to saw through his bindings, maybe more, but they had finally given way. The bitch of it all was he couldn't rotate his shoulders or move his arms for fear of someone walking in on him, yet every muscle in his body itched to do exactly that.

The enduring pain and waiting around game reminded him of his teenage training years. At the time, he'd hated every second of it since he'd never intended to be a sentry or soldier for the clan. Building things and figuring out how stuff worked had always fascinated him, and from a young age, Sean had known he wanted to study engineering. Yet right now, he was glad for the training since it was keeping him disciplined.

It might also keep him alive.

He'd been waiting for what seemed like hours for someone else to check on him and give him the chance to shift and escape, but so far, no one had come. Each second that ticked by squeezed his heart. Was Lauren okay? Had she already been placed into Purity's rehabilitation program? Would he ever see her again? And most importantly, would she want to see him again?

After all, she had every right to blame him for not thinking of her safety. Shifters were supposed to protect their prospective mates. Somehow, because of living in the human world for so many years now, he'd forgotten the most basic of rules in shifter life—to always remember that humans feared what was different, which meant each and every human could be your enemy.

Once he got out of this mess, he wouldn't be forgetting that detail again. If Lauren would still have him, it was time to move back to DarkStalker's lands in the mountains.

His cougar chirped at that. *I miss the mountains.*

Truth be told, so did he. He only hoped Lauren would be open to the idea. It would mean seeing her family less and adjusting to the shifter way of life.

Flexing his fingers behind his back, Sean focused back on his present situation. He could tell that his wounds on his palms had closed up and even healed a little. *Thank fuck for fast shifter healing.* Without it, his plan would probably fail.

The lock in the door clicked and he nearly jumped at the loudness of the sound after sitting so long in silence. This was it, his one and only chance at escape so he could find Lauren.

Cougar's First Christmas

His inner cougar growled. *We're ready. Shift and let me take care of them.*

Once the first human stepped inside the door, Sean swung his arms forward and let them become his front legs, his tail extended from his back, and his face shifted into a cougar's muzzle as his teeth elongated into fangs.

The whole process took less than five seconds, which was just enough time for surprise to knock up the heart rates of the three humans at the door.

Not wasting time, Sean let his inner animal take control and they bounded toward the humans. His cat wanted to kill, but Sean told him, *No. If we kill, we will lose Lauren. Knock them unconscious and then we go find her.*

With a reluctant growl, his cougar jumped on the first human at the door and the impact of the human's head smashing against the hard floor knocked the man unconscious.

One down, two to go.

He jumped to the next human and pinned her down with his paw against her neck to try to make her black out. In the wild, he would use his jaw around her neck to do the job, but a human's neck was a lot more delicate than a full grown stag deer.

Just as the woman stopped struggling, he finally noticed that the third human had run.

His cat growled out loud. *Good. I like the chase.*

Sean bounded down the hallway in his cougar-form, barely registering the cold, wet tiles under his paws. Unlike when he was in human-form, his paws prevented him from slipping on the slick surface.

As he ran full throttle, he kept his ears and nose open for sounds or scents of Lauren, but detected neither. Then he rounded the bend and came across the remaining human trying to punch in a code at a door. Sean slowed his run to stalk up behind the man who didn't seem to notice his approach.

Finding the last human so easily made him suspicious, but he pushed the feeling aside. Human Purity wasn't comprised of trained soldiers. It made sense that in small numbers they were easy to take down.

While a cougar in its prime could jump eighteen feet, city life had made him a little soft and Sean wasn't going to risk it. He waited until he was about six feet away before he jumped at the male human. Just as the force of his body smacked the human into the wall, sprinklers went off overhead.

Both cougar and human smashed to the floor. Ignoring the water raining down on him, Sean rolled the human male over, but he was relieved to see that the force had knocked him out cold. His inner cat wanted to teach at least one of the humans a lesson, but he told his cat no. *We need to find Lauren.*

With a reluctant hiss, his cougar allowed Sean to take control of their mind and he backed away from the human. Sean then imagined his paws turning into hands, his ears shrinking to human ones, and his tail merging back into his spine. Now a naked male, he crouched down, ripped the black mask off the male's face, and flipped him back over to tie his hands together.

All he wanted to do was rush to search each and every room in this place, but in the event Lauren had been moved, he needed the humans to stay put so he could interrogate them.

Satisfied the bindings would hold, Sean walked through the water pouring down on him and ran back to the other end of the building so he could tie up the remaining two humans. The water was pooling on the floor and he had to be careful not to slip. While letting his cougar out again would be easiest, he didn't want to waste precious time shifting. Who knew how long the other two humans would remain unconscious.

COUGAR'S FIRST CHRISTMAS

The two humans were still on the floor, now soaked from the sprinklers. He went to work removing their masks and tying their hands before moving them into his former room. Once the door clicked shut, Sean eyed the corridor of doors. Lauren could be behind any one of them.

He moved to the one directly across from his, but as he fiddled with the lock, his vision swam. He closed his eyes and opened them again, but that only made his vision blur worse.

What the fuck? What is happening to me?

His left leg went numb, and he knew something was wrong, but what? They hadn't injected him with anything in hours, nor had he eaten or drunk anything. Then the sound of the water pelting his skin made it all click together. These weren't ordinary sprinklers. No wonder the human male had been so keen to enter the code into that keypad. They had to be laced with some kind of drug.

Fuck. He needed a phone to call someone from his clan before he blacked out. No doubt one of the humans would have a cell phone.

As he turned and forced his heavy legs to move, he made it back inside the other room. But not two steps inside, all of a sudden, the room pitched beneath his feet, and Sean fell to his hands and knees.

He took a second to breathe in and out before trying to stand up again, but he experienced the same pitching sensation. On his third attempt, he said fuck it, and made his way over to the human female on the floor on his hands and knees. He quickly patted down her pockets, but he came up with nothing.

Shit. As his head started to pound in addition to the blurred vision and weird sense of balance, he pushed his body to move toward the other human. If he couldn't reach out to his clan, he wouldn't be able to help Lauren. She'd been drawn into this mess because of him. He wasn't about to abandon her.

Even if it took his last breath to find a way to save her, he'd do it.

He made it to the other human, but his balance went even more off-kilter, and he fell onto his stomach. Before he lost complete use of his arms, he reached out and felt the man's right pocket. Nothing. *Please let there be a phone in the other pocket.*

His strength was waning, but he inched over the man to feel the other side. His vision spotted as he felt around, but there was no rectangular object in the pocket. *Fuck.* He had no phone. There was no way to reach out to his clan, let alone Lauren. She would think he had abandoned her.

That thought made his heart squeeze. Even if he were dying right now, and he very well might be, that paled in comparison to the shame of failing his female. He'd been too cocky. Sean should've warned her and asked for his clan's help before this.

As his consciousness faded, all he could think about was how he'd fucked up for the sake of his pride instead of doing what was best for his female. Maybe it would be a good thing if he were dying because then she'd be free to find someone worthy of her.

He conjured up an image of her beautiful, deep brown face and warm brown eyes before he finally succumbed to the darkness.

CHAPTER SIX

Tapping her fingers against her leg, Lauren wondered what was taking so long. Their first location had been nothing more than an empty, abandoned warehouse. If Human Purity had once used it as a base, it'd been at least a few months since they'd stepped foot inside it.

Even with their first location a bust, Sy and his team were fairly confident about Sean being in the single-story building right outside the van. She hoped so. Her heart squeezed at the thought of spending weeks, months, or even years wondering if Sean were alive or dead. How would she move on without him?

Stop with the negativity, Lauren. Sean may still be alive.

She didn't like relying on strangers for help, especially since everyone seemed to think Sylas Murray was like a superhero and had zero doubts that he'd find Sean. All of that self-confidence made Lauren uneasy. After all, it was best to always prepare for the worst. Which, in her case, could mean raising a baby without a father.

She stared down at her stomach and tears prickled her eyes. If Sean were dead, the baby would be all she would have left of him. As much as she would love the little him or her, she had no idea how to raise a half-shifter child. Hell, she didn't even know if the child would be able to shift into a cougar.

When it came to shifters, all of Lauren's education meant nothing. She felt like a child on her first day of school.

The voice of Dr. Lisa, who had asked her to just call her Lisa, interrupted her thoughts. "Sylas Murray saved our entire clan a few months ago. He's got this, Lauren. If Sean is alive, he will find him."

Lauren glanced over at the shifter woman. "I want to believe in him, but surely you've seen the videos Purity released in the past. They've refined their torture to make it last."

"It's sick, I agree. But while Sean is an engineer and spends most of his days inside an office, he had self-defense and combat training as a teenager. All shifters do, both male and female."

"Even you?"

Lisa smiled. "Yes, even me. Although it's been over a decade since I've used any of it. I spend most of my time in the lab. Of course, after this, I might have to get back into practice."

In a normal situation, Lauren would be curious and ask more about what Lisa did for research. Or, ask about the shifter training and see if she could complete it too. Yet right now, she felt about as social as a worm. All she could think about was Sean.

The female shifter's phone vibrated, and Lauren's heart skipped a beat. "Is it Sy? What did he say?"

Rather than waste time answering her, Lisa stared at her phone and then typed something before looking back to Lauren. "They found him. Sean's alive, but unconscious."

A small thrill of joy rushed through her body, but as Lisa reached behind her for her doctor's bag, Lauren had a feeling she hadn't heard the whole truth. "What aren't you telling me?"

"Sy isn't sure, but one of the wolves with him is a trained biological scientist, and he thinks they've drugged him with something."

"Is it life threatening?"

"We don't know. Whatever it was, it was absorbed through the skin."

While part of Lauren appreciated the shifter's honesty, her words made her stomach drop. "Is there anything I can do?"

"Not yet. First, we'll have to transport him separately to make sure he's not infected with anything airborne. If he's cleared from airborne transmission, then until we get him somewhere safe and wash him off, you're not to touch him without gloves, do you understand?"

She put out her hands. "Then give me some gloves."

Lisa gave a half smile. "No whining and protesting. I like you more and more, human."

She shrugged one shoulder. "There's a lot about your kind I don't know, and I'm not about to presume otherwise. My whining and weeping won't help my man."

"Just prepare yourself. As much as I admire your fortitude, it may slip when you see him."

Lisa crawled between the seats to sit in the driver's seat and a sense of panic built in Lauren's stomach. "We're leaving him?"

"My job is to get you to safety. Sy has things in hand and will move Sean to a secure location for testing."

Curses were on the tip of her tongue, but Lauren resisted the urge. This shifter female was just trying to help her.

When she was sure she could talk normally, she said, "How long until I can see him?"

The doctor started the car. "I'm taking you to the same facility, albeit in a different wing. GreyFire Industries has a research facility we lease nearby. As soon as every test imaginable is run on your male, I'll take you to him myself. While waiting, we can confirm your pregnancy as well."

As Lisa pulled out onto the road, Lauren closed her eyes and sent good thoughts toward her shifter. At least she now knew he was alive. It was only a matter of time before she discovered for how long.

~~~

Five hours later, Lauren watched as yet another doctor entered the room on the other side of the observation window. Her fiancée lay on a table, unconscious in his cat form. His tan fur was matted, and his body was limp in a way that seemed "off"; he was far too still. Even when he slept in cat form, he'd move every once in a while, not unlike how domestic cats would make soft noises or twitch a paw in response to their dreams.

Yet for the last four or so hours she'd been allowed to watch, he hadn't twitched once.

Clenching a fist in front of her heart, she tried not to cry. She'd been strong up until now, but her exhaustion from the ordeal and the now-confirmed pregnancy was pushing her closer and closer to her breaking point.

"Sean," she whispered, "I need you."

She knew it was selfish, but even just being in the same room as him would ease the fears that had been building minute by minute.

The door behind her opened and she turned to see Lisa carrying a clipboard. Lauren didn't miss a beat. "Well? Did they find anything?"

"No."

"Does that mean I can go see him?"

For a second, Lisa stared at her and Lauren braced herself for another denial, but then the shifter female smiled, and hope bubbled in her chest. Lisa said, "You really do love him, don't you?"

Giving her a look of irritation, she answered, "Of course I do. Now tell me if I can see Sean or not."

60

"All right, all right. I do have good news and bad. The good news is that he doesn't have anything that is airborne, which means you can see him."

Lauren clapped her hands together. "Then let's go."

The doctor put up a hand. "Not just yet. You need to know that we're still trying to pinpoint what's wrong. So you're wearing gloves until I give the all clear."

"Fine, fine. I'll wear a pink tutu if it means I get to be in the same room as Sean."

Lisa gave her a long look before she nodded. "Okay, follow me."

They walked down a utilitarian hallway with white walls and black and white tiles on the floor. After making three turns and entering through a door Lisa opened with a code, they stood in a small room with another observation window.

Sean was on the other side, much closer than from her previous vantage point, and was not more than fifteen feet away.

Blinking back tears, Lauren took the gloves offered her, put them on, and looked to Lisa. The other woman nodded, punched a code, and the door opened. She gestured with a hand. "Go talk to your future mate and convince him to wake up."

Not needing any encouragement, Lauren rushed past the doctor and went straight to Sean's side.

She reached out a hand and brushed the top of his head until she could scratch behind his ears as she said, "Sean, babe, it's me. Christmas is almost over. Wake up, so I can tell you about your other present."

Yet the cougar under her fingers remained both still and silent.

As she continued to stroke his head, his back, and his legs, she told him about waking up from the accident, calling his clan leader, and meeting the other shifters. Then she said, "So in case you haven't noticed by now, I can handle your clan. Wake up for me, babe, and I'll say yes to being your mate and move to DarkStalker's land if you want. I think our children will do best there, surrounded by love."

Beyond the rise and fall of his chest for breathing, Sean didn't move. She wanted to kiss his cute pink and black nose since that had always been a surefire way to wake him up in the past, but she wouldn't ignore Lisa's warning about touching him. Instead, she bopped his nose with a gloved finger before pulling the nearby chair close and sitting down. She took Sean's giant paw in her hands, and braced herself to wait.

~ ~ ~

Lauren had been dozing, but she was awake enough to register Lisa's voice over the intercom. "Stay still, Lauren, and keep your eyes shut. Sean's waking up and we don't know what kind of state he'll be in."

It took everything she had to not open her eyes. If Sean's animal half was in charge and wild like the others had warned her about, then making eye contact could be fatal. No, it was best to remain still and control her breathing until her next set of instructions.

Yet as the seconds ticked by, she grew nervous. If Sean were awake and conscious, he would've made some sort of noise to get her attention.

Come on, babe, say something.

But it wasn't Sean's meow she heard but rather Lisa's voice again. "He's staring at you and sniffing the air. Open your eyes slowly. If you see recognition in his eyes, let me know. Otherwise, talk to him in a soothing voice to try to get his human-half to recognize you and come to the forefront of his mind."

Lisa hadn't given her a reason not to trust her, so with a slow inhalation, Lauren opened her eyes. A pair of light-blue cougar eyes stared at her. Searching his eyes, there was no recognition there, just curiosity and confusion.

Remembering what Lisa had told her when confirming her pregnancy, Lauren had an idea as to why, so she said in a soothing voice, "Right now, you don't know who I am, but my scent is confusing you because you can smell your own scent mixed with mine." The cougar merely stared. Lauren forced aside her sadness at the love of her life not recognizing her and decided to push a little further. "Your scent is part of me because, Sean Fisher, I'm carrying your child."

Sean in cougar-form tilted his head. *He's not convinced yet.* "I'm going to raise my arm for you to get a better whiff, okay? Then you'll really be able to smell the mixture of scents."

Before Lisa could tell her not to do it, Lauren slowly raised her arm until it was about six inches from the cougar's nose. Despite how much she believed in her shifter, her heart was racing. One of Lisa's theories about the drug used on Sean was that it would chemically damage a shifter's brain in such a way that only the animal side could take control.

Meaning, she might never get her man back.

No. She wasn't about to give up just yet.

Her patience paid off as the cougar leaned closer and sniffed her arm. His nose even touched the sleeve of her shirt. Hopefully, the material would be enough to protect her just in case she could catch whatever Sean had.

The big cat sniffed up her arm until it reached her neck. A small flash of fear shot through her body at that powerful jaw so close to her own, but she quickly pushed it aside. If she didn't believe in Sean, then who would? Keeping still, she said, "The scent is strongest where my neck meets my shoulder. Take a deep sniff, kitty cat, and when your animal instincts recognize I'm telling the truth, allow the human half back in control." She turned her head slightly to meet the cougar's intense blue gaze. "I need him to help protect our baby. Please."

She swore she saw something flash in the cat's eyes, but Lauren didn't want to get her hopes up. Remaining logical and collected was her best chance at bringing Sean back.

Since the room was dead quiet, the sound of the cougar sniffing her neck was especially loud. Normally, she loved it when he sniffed her neck in cat form before licking her jaw. The thought of Sean never doing that again squeezed her heart.

As the cat continued to breathe in her scent, all Lauren could do was wait and hope for the best.

CHAPTER SEVEN

Sean was a prisoner inside his own body. He instinctively knew he was awake, yet all he saw was blackness. A few times in the past, when he'd been gravely injured, his cougar had taken control and pushed him to the back of their mind to force him to rest and heal.

Yet this time was different. Unlike in the past when his cat would chirp or meow back at him when he mentally reached out to his cougar, whenever he tried to take control of his brain, his cougar snarled and pushed him back. It was almost as if his own inner cougar saw him as an enemy.

No doubt, all of this had to do with that drug they'd sprayed on him. Since his human brain, albeit confined, seemed to be working, he needed to think of a plan.

But before he had thought of anything that might work, he caught Lauren's faint scent in his nose. Was she nearby? He hoped like hell his cat hadn't hurt her or he'd never forgive himself.

Again, he tried to shove the darkness away to take control of his brain, but his cat growled back at him.

Fuck. If his cougar was acting that way with him, he was afraid of how it would act with Lauren since she was human.

A stronger wave of Lauren's scent reached him, but this time he noticed something—his scent was mixed with hers. While faint, it was still there, which meant only one thing: Lauren was pregnant with his child.

Roaring inside his own mind, he again tried to push away his confinement. Not only did he need to protect his female, he also had his unborn child to take care of. He needed to reach both before Human Purity took their little one away from them.

With a roar, he mentally pushed against the wall keeping him in. The darkness parted for a second and he caught a small glimpse of Lauren sitting next to him, but then the blackness returned. The small glimpse told him she was alive and offering him her neck. How did she know her scent might help bring his human-half back or that it was strongest there? He didn't recall ever sharing that tidbit of information about shifters.

He was hit with another wave of Lauren's scent mixed with his, and he mentally growled at his cat. *You can't protect her alone. She needs both of us. Let me free.*

His cat ignored him.

The bastard. Well, if the animal half of him wasn't going to listen, he'd just have to force his way out.

True, he could mentally go too far and burn out both him and his cougar, but it wasn't like Sean had a choice. If he couldn't get free of his prison, he couldn't help his female, let alone protect her.

Gathering what strength he had left, he mentally pushed against his invisible wall. Thinking of never seeing Lauren or their child ever again, he grew stronger, drawing even more from his remaining energy, and pushed harder.

Something happened because suddenly the darkness was gone, and he could see out of his eyes in cougar form. Lauren was in front of him, her heart racing, and giving off a slight scent of fear.

She was afraid of him.

He was exhausted, but he used the last of his mental energy to shove his inner cat to the back of his mind and into a temporary prison at the same time as he imagined his body shifting into a human. Maybe this way Lauren would know it was him and not his cat in charge.

He must have succeeded as he now felt the cold steel of the table under his ass, but before he could reach for Lauren, the world went black.

~~~

It took a second for Lauren to process Sean's shift, but the instant his human hand went limp and his eyes closed, she jumped up and placed a gloved hand on his chest. "Babe, talk to me."

He didn't respond.

Before she could yell for help, Lisa was on the opposite side of the table. The temptation to ask what was wrong was strong, but she resisted; wasting even one second could mean game over for her man.

She merely watched as Lisa checked his pulse at his neck, reached for something out of the bag she'd brought in with her, and faced back toward Lauren with a syringe in her hand. The next second, the needle was in Sean's neck.

As the doctor pushed the plunger, Lauren took Sean's hand and squeezed. She had no idea what was going on, but she trusted Lisa to do all that she could in the moment and explain the how and why of it later.

A few other shifters came into the room and pushed her out of the way. One of the women told her to go back to the observation room. Lauren didn't want to leave, but she'd dealt with her own share of crazy parents who'd had to be kicked out of the room while she worked on their children's teeth, so with one last glance, she retreated into the smaller observation room.

Despite the two-way mirror, she rarely caught more than a glimpse of Sean's arm or leg over the next thirty minutes. By the time Lisa came into the room, Lauren was clenching her hands so hard they were more cream than brown. "Well? How is he?"

"He's stable for now. Sean suffered a mental burn out. It happens sometimes when the human and animal halves fight against each other."

"Will he be okay?"

"That depends. Usually with adult shifters, they regain consciousness fifteen to thirty minutes after blacking out and end up recovering in full. But due to the unknown drugs in his system, I'm not exactly sure what will happen."

The door opened behind them and Lauren turned to find a man who looked a lot like Sylas with the same dark hair and green eyes, but whereas Sy had a cocky swagger, this man limped. But no matter what was wrong with his leg, his face was all business. Lisa said, "Kian."

Without thinking, she blurted out, "You're Kian Murray, as in DarkStalker's leader?"

The corner of Kian's mouth ticked up and he looked more like Sylas. "That would be me, Lauren Spencer. Sy told me all about you." He looked to Lisa. "How's Sean? Have we figured out what's wrong with him yet?"

Lisa recounted the basics of Sean's case, including her latest news of his mental burn out. Then Kian said, "Sy and some of my clan members have been interrogating the Human Purity members Sean tied up back at that abandoned building, but nothing useful has come out yet. They'll call me the second they know anything. For now, just do your best." Kian looked to Lauren. "You and I need to talk."

For a split second, she wanted to reach out to Lisa and ask her to stay, but then Lauren remembered that once she was Sean's mate, this shifter male would be her clan leader too. How she acted now would dictate their future relationship.

Provided, of course, he allowed for them to live on DarkStalker's land. It was illegal to permanently house a human on shifter land, and Kian might think she and Sean were too much trouble and send them away.

Kian nodded to Lisa and the woman went back into the room with Sean, leaving her alone with the tall, muscled shifter male. He scrutinized her for a second before saying, "I've known about you for a while, Lauren, and know everything I need to know for the decision I'm about to make. Listen to my proposition, and then I'll give you the chance to back out. Sound fair?"

A normal human might be afraid of the cougar-shifter leader, whose very voice seemed to make her want to listen to him, but she wasn't about to cower. "I don't know if it's fair or not until I hear what you have to say."

Kian smiled. "You remind me a little of my mate." His face became more serious. "I've found a way for you to legally live on my land."

She blinked. "What? How?"

"Well, I should say that one of the ShadowClaw lawyers thinks they found a way, although I'm sure your human courts will test it."

Her heart thumped in her chest. If there was a legal way for her to be with Sean and his clan, she'd never heard about it before. "Then hurry up and tell me what it is."

"Sy was right about you. Anyway, the loophole exists because you're pregnant with Sean's cub."

She frowned. "I don't follow."

"Well, as long as you carry his cub, you carry shifter DNA. The laws state only those with shifter DNA can legally marry another with shifter DNA. The ShadowClaw bears told me it was written that way because there were always half-shifters running around, and the US government didn't want them marrying humans and spreading the genes."

"But once the baby is born, I'll be one-hundred percent human again. And as much as I love Sean, it's not like I want to carry one baby after another just to meet the requirements of this law."

"I have a whole clan of bear-shifter lawyers willing to help me defend your case, so that's not the issue. However, if you do agree, you will have to live on my land. And until I say it's safe enough to leave, you'll be trapped in the mountains for the foreseeable future. Whatever your decision, I'm afraid I need it now."

"Before I can even discuss it with Sean?"

Kian nodded. "As soon as Lisa gives the okay, we're moving Sean back to the mountains. If you plan on coming, we need to move quickly to make the necessary preparations."

Lauren turned around to look at Sean through the glass. He was still unconscious in his human-form. She wished with her whole heart he would wake up so she could discuss this. Sure, he had proposed to her yesterday—had it only been yesterday?—but a lot had changed since then. Would he feel cornered if she said yes? Not only that, there was the matter of her family. Turning back toward Kian, she asked, "And what about my friends and family? Will I ever be able to see them again?"

"I'm not going to lie to you, so I'm going to say I don't know. If they pass the checks and can be trusted, then maybe. Usually Purity doesn't go after family members since they're focused solely on those having sex with shifters, but their tactics keep changing, which makes them unpredictable."

The thought of her family being in danger because of her decision squeezed her heart. "Then if that does happen, could my family move onto DarkStalker's land?"

He studied her a second and she feared she'd gone too far. Then Kian shook his head as he answered, "Why do I get the feeling you'd keep trying to bargain with me until I said yes?"

Hope bubble in her chest. "Well, I always fight for those I love. Surely, as clan leader, you understand that trait all too well."

Kian smiled and Lauren knew she'd won. "Fine. As long as they check out and we can confirm they're not a threat and don't mind disappearing from the rest of the world, then yes, we'll find a way to sneak them onto my land. But until that threat is certain, we'll see about arrangements. Your family has been your own clan, and I don't want to deny you access to them if I can help it."

Lauren clapped her hands together. "Yeah. Good. Then with those terms, I want to marry Sean and become part of your clan. I'll set up a dental practice, and I'll get to learn more about your interesting teeth."

Kian was about to say something when Lisa barged into the room saying, "Sean's awake. Lauren, we need you."

At Lisa's words, the light atmosphere of the room vanished. Lauren nodded and followed the doctor into the room. She grabbed a pair of gloves on her way in, and the other shifters in the room moved so she could see Sean. Despite the paleness of his face and the fatigue in his eyes, he was awake. When her eyes met his, he smiled and said, "Lauren."

Sean felt like his body had been dragged on the road behind a car for ten miles. He was so weak that he could barely move a finger, let alone a leg. The faces of his clan, and even some of the wolves, sent a flush of relief through his body; he was no longer a Human Purity captive.

However, there was one face missing. Ignoring the questions being thrown his way, his voice was weak to his own ears when he said, "Where's Lauren?"

Lisa, the GreyFire wolves' head medical researcher, pushed to his side and said, "I'll get her, but first, I need to know if you have your cougar under control. I won't risk her safety."

He remembered trapping the cat in the back of his mind, but he did a check and mentally sent out a question. *Are you better now?*

His inner cougar chirped, so Sean allowed the cat a little more free rein. His cougar hesitated before mentally reaching out to him and giving another chirp. Sean could tell his cat was back to normal, and sad that they had frightened their female.

Aware that his cougar's behavior had been a result of the drugs, Sean sent thoughts of forgiveness to his cat before he looked back to Lisa. "He's fine now. Whatever you did while I was unconscious returned him back to normal."

Lisa studied him a second before nodding. "Good. Let my colleagues do a once-over while I go get Lauren."

The wolf doctor disappeared. As her colleagues checked his temperature and did a quick exam, he vaguely remembered Lauren's scent giving him the strength to regain control. Wait, not just her scent, but his as well.

That's right; she was carrying his child.

COUGAR'S FIRST CHRISTMAS

Neither one had planned on it happening, but he couldn't help but feel a small thrill of joy at the prospect of a child. And not just any child, one made by him and Lauren.

Before his doubts about their future could take hold, the love of his life was at his side. She placed a gloved hand on his forehead. As she stroked him, her eyes filled with tears. She whispered, "Sean, is it true? Are you okay?"

He gave a weak smile, wishing he had the strength to wrap his female in his arms and reassure her with his touch. Instead, he said, "I'm not going to lie. I feel like shit right now, but it's nothing I can't lick." A tear slid down Lauren's cheek and his heart squeezed. "Baby, please don't cry. Somehow we'll be fine. We always find a way to make it work."

"I know, but, Sean, so much is happening and I don't even know where to begin. I only have a few minutes with you before you're supposed to rest again."

"Then let's cut to the chase. Was it a hallucination, or are you pregnant, love?"

His female's eyes widened. "So you remember?" He gave a slight nod, and she continued, "It was unplanned, but I swear I was going to tell you. It was my second Christmas gift to you."

Even through his tiredness, his humor refused to sit by the wayside. "Considering how shitty my first Christmas has been thus far, I'll take whatever I can get to make it better."

His humor worked, and Lauren gave him a playful smack on the chest. "Our baby is worth much more than 'whatever I can get', Sean Fisher. Keep on like that, and I'll have more than enough stories to make me the favorite parent of the two."

He smiled. "I can live with that since it means you're sticking around."

He said it in a lighthearted way, but in reality, it took everything he had not to hold his breath as he waited for Lauren's reaction. Just because she seemed to want their baby didn't mean she wanted to stay with him after the scare he'd given earlier.

Especially since he still didn't know if she'd been taken by Human Purity.

Then she smiled and it wiped away most of his fears. "Since Kian found a way for us to marry that might be legal, yes, I'm sticking around."

He might be exhausted, but he was awake enough to make the connection. "So you're saying yes to being my mate?"

"If you still want me, then yes, Sean Fisher, I'll be your mate."

Before he could think better of it, he added, "Even though I failed you with Human Purity? You still want me despite that?"

She frowned. "Human Purity only took you, not me. I was left in the car. I used your cell phone to call Kian, and, well, the rest of that story can wait for later. Just know that I've come to like the shifters I've met so far."

He let out a sigh of relief. "Thank fuck. When I was trapped, all I could think about was getting to you before they tried to rehabilitate you."

"Nope, if anything, I'm more of a shifter lover than ever before. Especially for this one shifter, who still hasn't said anything about me accepting his offer."

She wants to be my mate. Happiness warmed his entire body. "I'm sort of pro-human myself. This one woman has sort of ruined me for all others."

Lauren laughed, making her whole face light up. The sight took his breath away. "I wish I could kiss the living shit out of you right now, but it's going to have to wait, baby. I hope you don't mind."

"As long as you make it worth it, babe, I can wait."

74

COUGAR'S FIRST CHRISTMAS

Lisa cleared her throat and interjected, "Felicitations on your upcoming mating, but it's time to let Sean rest and put your transport to DarkStalker's land into motion."

Never taking his eyes from Lauren's warm, brown-eyed gaze, he said, "Just as long as Lauren is with me, I'll follow your instructions to the letter."

Lauren laughed. "Don't believe him, Lisa. Following instructions is not a habit of his."

Lisa moved to stand next to Lauren. "Shifter males rarely do, until their mates start withholding sex. That usually gets them agreeable fast, isn't that right, Kian?"

In all of the commotion with Lauren saying yes to being his mate, Sean hadn't sensed his clan leader. With great effort, he forced his gaze from Lauren to Kian Murray just as his leader sighed. "You're not supposed to share that secret so early." His leader met his eyes. "Sorry, Sean, but it's only going to get worse from here. Just wait until Trinity tracks her down and starts giving her 'shifter lessons.' A newborn baby will seem a welcome distraction by then."

Kian's words were more than him teasing Sean; they were an acknowledgement. His clan leader was going to treat Lauren as one of their own.

Looking back to Lauren, Sean said, "But waiting can make it that much sweeter, as Lauren well knows."

She swatted his chest and whispered, "Sean."

He grinned. He might have to wait a week or so to recover, but Lauren would always be worth the wait.

Always.

CHAPTER EIGHT

Two weeks later

The cut on Lauren's palm stung like hell, but with each stroke of Sean's tongue against hers, the pain faded.

Even when he broke their kiss, the heated look in his eyes made her shiver. If they weren't standing in front of the entire clan, she would be asking him to strip. Not just because they'd just been mated, but also because Sean had only been cleared for sex that day and she was more than ready for him to take her anyway he could think of.

Sean growled and whispered, "Stop it. Your arousal is making it hard for me to control my cougar, and the last thing I want is to have a hard-on when meeting your parents for the first time."

Lauren smiled. "It's not my fault your clan took so long to get them here."

"Sneaking humans onto our land isn't exactly legal, baby."

"I know." Someone cleared their throat to her left and she saw Kian. He must've climbed the stairs to the dais during their kiss. "Is there something we're supposed to do next?"

DarkStalker's leader shook his head. "No, but if I don't guide you out of this room right now to the one where your parents have gone to wait for you, you'll have hundreds of shifters trying to congratulate and tease you about your honeymoon period and you won't see your parents until well after midnight."

She leaned against Sean's shoulder and his free hand went around her waist. She said, "Thanks, Kian. All of this is probably a shock to my parents, and some privacy will be good."

Kian nodded. "Okay, then let's go. Mating ceremonies are celebrated hard in our clan, and the sooner you talk with your parents, the sooner you can join in the fun."

She wasn't sure everyone would be celebrating. A few of the cougar-shifters were skeptical of her presence. Only because of their love of Kian did they accept her, but she hoped it would change in time.

As they maneuvered through the crowd, Kian deflected everyone who tried to talk with them. Well, except for when Sylas Murray and his mate, Kaya Alexie, managed to shove him aside. Sy grinned and squeezed the tall, beautiful woman frowning at his side. Kaya said, "Sylas, Kian is clearly trying to get them out of this room. Despite what you may think, you are not the most important person in the world."

Sy looked to Lauren. "Pay no attention to my mate. In private, she acknowledges how awesome I am. Usually, she's naked and does so in many creative ways too, not just with words."

Kaya smacked his side and Lauren smiled. She looked to the wolf-shifter clan leader and remembered what Kian's mate had told her to say when meeting Kaya for the first time. "While I know you're Kaya, we haven't officially met. I'm Lauren Spencer-Fisher. And just to let you know, Sy was very close to flirting with me when we first met. What was it he said? Ah, yes, that if he didn't have you as a mate, he might try to steal me away."

Sean growled. "He said what? You never mentioned that."

She bit her lip. "You were recovering."

"Sylas Murray, if you hit on my mate again, I'll challenge you to a fight."

Kaya raised an eyebrow. "Sean is the least of your worries, Sy. You hit on Lauren again and you won't like what I'll do to your favorite appendage."

As Sy tried to dig himself out of the hole he'd created, Kian rolled his eyes and said, "Forgive my stupid twin and follow me."

Sensing Sean's possessiveness, she leaned against him as they moved toward the far exit. "Sean, babe, it's okay. I'm yours and only yours."

He grunted. "I know, but with the baby and the mating, my cougar doesn't like the image of charming Sylas Murray hitting on you."

"I'm yours, babe. Sy might be charming, but you're my mate. I love you."

Sean relaxed at her side and she knew her words were working. Wrangling a possessive cougar was no easy task, but since the possessiveness would worsen as her pregnancy progressed, this was good practice.

Of course, as they approached the far exit, Sean's jealousy paled in comparison to the flips her stomach was doing. While she'd chatted with her parents over the phone and via webcam with Sean at her side, this was the first time they'd be meeting in person. Getting them onto DarkStalker's land had been hard enough; now she had the monumental task of ensuring they'd want to come back, especially once the baby came.

Stop it, Lauren. They'll love him like you do. Repeating that thought in her mind, they exited the great hall and entered a nearby room.

~~~

COUGAR'S FIRST CHRISTMAS

Sean's cougar was pacing inside his head. Partly because of Sylas Murray's actions, but also because of Lauren being out and exposed in public while carrying their baby.

He sent soothing thoughts to his inner cat. *It's not like we can lock her up for the next eight months. Calm the fuck down.*

Since all his cougar did was snarl, he pushed the beast into the back of his mind as they approached the door to one of Kian's private meeting rooms.

His mate's heartbeat was racing, so he squeezed her waist. "Don't worry, baby, it'll be fine."

She glanced up at him and smiled. "It'd better be. I faced a group of cougar-shifters on my own and won them over, surely two humans can't be that hard."

He winked. "I'm not as charming as Sy, but I'll try my best."

Leaning into him, she whispered, "Just don't make any sex jokes or innuendos. That won't go over well."

He barked out a laugh. "I'll keep that in mind."

Kian shot them a glance before opening the door and ushering them inside. The clan leader half-turned away as he said, "Sean knows the way, so come join us when you're ready." He looked over at Lauren's parents. "We'd be honored if you joined us too, Mr. and Mrs. Spencer."

The tall, middle-aged man with skin darker than Lauren's nodded. "Thank you, Mr. Murray."

Then Kian was gone and they were alone.

Giving his mate one last squeeze, he approached the middle-aged couple and put out his hand without the mating cut. "Nice to meet you, Mr. Spencer."

Lauren's father was nearly as tall as Sean and had a sprinkling of gray mixed into his short, curly hair. His eyes, however, reminded Sean of Lauren's, and right now, those deep brown eyes were assessing him. Her father finally took his hand and shook. "Did you mean what you said, during the 'mating ceremony'?"

He stood tall. "Yes. I would give my life to protect your daughter. She is my everything. Well, at least until the baby comes; then they both will be."

Lauren's whisper of, "Oh, Sean," reached his ears and he barely resisted returning to her side. He needed to sort out where he stood with her parents and wouldn't use his female to hide behind.

Mr. Spencer then looked to his daughter. "Baby girl, all I need to know is if you're truly happy with this man. Because if you're not, then just say the word and I'll knock him flat on his ass. I may be out of practice, but in my army days, I was a pretty good boxer."

Of course he had been. Sean knew about the army side of things, but not the boxing.

Still, for Lauren, he'd fight anyone if it would make her happy.

Lauren cleared her throat. "Daddy, how many times do I have to tell you I love Sean? Imagine your life without Mama. I'd feel the same way without Sean."

Lauren's mother rolled her eyes and let out a sigh. "Give it a rest, James. Our baby could send you fifteen texts a day saying she loves her shifter, and you'd still not believe her." The plump woman pushed aside her husband and surprised Sean with a hug. Her voice was muffled against his shoulder. "Welcome to the family, Sean. Seeing you with my baby up on that stage, there was no denying the love shining in both of your eyes."

As Sean gave an awkward pat to Mrs. Spencer's shoulder, Lauren's father grunted and said, "For now, welcome to the family, but if you hurt our little girl, my son and I will hunt your ass down and make you pay."

Rather than argue how Sean would probably win, he merely said, "Yes, sir."

Mrs. Spencer released him and patted his cheek. "Okay, now that my husband has gotten his threats out of his system, how about you and my daughter introduce us to everyone? I've never seen so many shifters in my life, and I must admit, it's a little exciting. They're all so tall and attractive."

Lauren was at his side. "Mama!"

Mrs. Spencer shrugged. "What? Surely you've noticed how good-looking they all are." She turned to her husband. "None compare to your father, of course."

Glancing down, Sean could tell Lauren was fighting a laugh. "Of course."

Mr. Spencer grunted again. "Let's go back to the party. Your mother hasn't stopped talking about the shifters, and I'm hoping she'll get her fill so I don't have to hear about it all the way home."

Mrs. Spencer clapped her hands, much like Lauren did when she was excited. "Michael couldn't come today, but I'll bring him soon. Then I can maybe see more of their land."

Lauren laughed and Sean finally let loose his smile. As her parents bantered, he reached out and pulled his mate close so he could whisper, "I think your mother likes me for my hotness."

After giving a mock slap, Lauren said, "I don't need to hear about my mother lusting after you."

"Oh, I don't know; it's kind of funny to watch you when you're embarrassed."

Lauren stood on her tip-toes and murmured into his ear, "The sooner we get them back to the party, the sooner we can sneak back to our room."

Sean had done a pretty good job of keeping his lust in check, but now all he could think about was his mate naked under him, moaning his name.

His inner cat perked up at that fantasy, and Sean knew his time was limited. He whispered, "Then let's get back to the party, ASAP."

Lauren laughed before herding her parents out of the room. As he watched his mate walking between her parents, he couldn't stop staring at her ass. He needed her naked, and he needed her now.

CHAPTER NINE

Sean did one last sweep with his eyes before he whispered, "Now's our chance."

He moved out of DarkStalker's grand meeting space, tugging Lauren behind him as he went down one corridor and then another. Smart female that his mate was, she had her heels in hand so she could keep up with him.

After what seemed like forever, they finally reached their new quarters inside DarkStalker's living area. He opened the door and said, "Shifter tradition decrees we kiss before entering and then spend the next three days having wild, kinky sex."

Lauren raised an eyebrow. "Decrees? Really? That word tells me all I need to know. I call bullshit."

He shrugged as he gave her body a long, slow once-over, loving how the silky, cream-colored dress fit her breasts and hips. "Hey, I've spent the last two hours imagining every way I could get you out of that dress. Making up a shifter tradition was just my first strategy."

She quirked an eyebrow. "And what was the second?"

He tugged until her body was pressed against his. He nuzzled her cheek as he said, "Toying with my prey until she begs me to fuck her." He nipped her jaw and his mate's heart rate kicked up. "You'll be squirming before long, all but begging for my tongue and cock. At that point, you'll forget all about your mating dress."

He felt her softening, but his mate would never give in easily. She ran a hand down his back until she gripped his right ass cheek. "I have a better idea."

"Oh?"

A slow, sexy smile spread across her face. "How about you unwrap me like you did on Christmas?"

"Baby, my first step in unwrapping you at Christmas was to take you against the wall while you were still dressed. There's no way I can fuck you in that tight dress and not rip it."

She ran a hand up from his ass to the skin at the back of his neck and whispered, "Then improvise, but save the dress. I might pass it down to our baby."

At the mention of their child, Sean squeezed her tighter. "You're so sure the baby is a girl, but if it's a boy, I'm not sure he'd appreciate the dress."

She laughed. "Then we'll just have to keep trying until we have a girl."

"I think we need lots and lots of practice, just to make sure we know what we're doing. The first time might've just been a fluke."

"I'll deconstruct that excuse later. For now, if it'll make you kiss me faster, I'll go with it."

He grinned before he cupped her face and placed a gentle kiss on her lips. "There. How's that?"

"If that's all you've got, then maybe I should see if there's a shifter-equivalent of an annulment."

The thought of Lauren leaving him made his inner cougar growl. *Don't hesitate. Fuck her hard and brand her.*

Rather than argue with his cougar about how she already carried his scent because of the baby, he cupped Lauren's cheek and whispered, "You asked for it," before he lowered his lips to hers and pushed his tongue into her mouth.

84

He distantly heard her heels drop to the floor before she laced her hands behind his neck. The feeling of her soft skin against his made him growl, and he continued to nip her lips and devour her mouth as he walked them into the room.

The hard points of her nipples were pressed against his chest, and all he could think about was sucking them deep into his mouth. But some small part of him remembered his promise, so he broke the kiss. His voice was husky when he said, "Take off the dress while I lock the door."

He moved to the door, shut it, and locked it. As he turned around, he yanked his tie over his head, stripped off his jacket, and moved to the buttons of his dress shirt. Why the fuck had he agreed to wear a suit? He needed to be naked and inside his mate.

Deciding the shirt wasn't anything special, he ripped it open, the buttons flying every which way, before he shucked off his shoes. His pants quickly followed suit.

When he looked up, Lauren was leaning over the back of the couch, her breasts dangling in front of her. She raised an eyebrow. "I'm waiting."

He'd ask how she'd undressed so quickly later. Right now, just looking at her breasts and dark nipples made his cock throb with need and let out a drop of precum.

He moved behind her and stroked her back with his hands before reaching around and cupping her small, soft breasts. The pregnancy had already left them swollen, but the thought of his female showing physical signs of carrying his child only made warmth spread through his body.

Massaging her breasts, he rubbed his dick against her soft, full ass as he said, "Shifters do like it from behind. How about pleasing the cat before I take my time to devour you properly?"

He pinched her nipples and Lauren rubbed her soft ass against his dick. "Stop talking already and fuck me, Sean."

~~~

Lauren had designed her mating dress to be easy to slip out of on purpose. Sean had spent most of the last two weeks first recovering and then being cleared of any possible diseases or infections. The whole time, they'd had to abstain. Lauren had only been able to touch his skin again a few days ago.

As a result, it might have been wrong with her parents always nearby during the mating ceremony and celebration, but Lauren had been thinking about Sean's long, hard cock pounding into her from behind all evening.

For some reason, being pregnant made her extremely horny. She blamed it on the half-shifter baby inside her; shifters were more sexual and demanding than humans, after all.

Then Sean pinched her nipples again as he lightly bit her shoulder, and she forgot about everything but the man behind her. "Sean."

Biting harder, he pressed his hard, warm chest against her back, and she loved the feel of his scraggly hairs against her skin. She felt his breath on her ear as he murmured, "Let's make sure you're nice and wet for me, baby."

She rubbed her ass against his cock. She smiled at the answering hiss.

But her smile faded as she felt his big, rough fingers plunge into her pussy without warning. Judging by the thickness, it was three of them.

Sean retreated and fucked her with his fingers a few more times, each thrust a wonderful sensation against her nerves. Then he removed his fingers and she let out a sound of protest at the sudden emptiness; she'd missed any part of him being inside her over the last two weeks.

She growled, and he chuckled before kissing her neck. "My mate is nice and wet for me."

"Wet and frustrated as hell. Fuck me now, Sean Fisher, or I'll unpack the vibrator."

Without a word, he thrust his cock into her and she arched her back. His voice was like a whisper against her neck. "No vibrator. Tonight you're mine, all mine."

That she could live with.

Then he gripped her hips with his warm hands and started thrusting in and out of her, slowly at first, before picking up speed. Only because of her grip on the couch in front of her could she remain standing.

Sean then changed his angle, and his pounding went from good to fabulous. Without thinking, she hummed and said, "Harder."

The sound of flesh slapping against flesh filled the room, and she gripped the couch as she arched her back. She loved the way his big cock fit inside her. Then he slapped her ass and she moaned. Maybe later he'd tie her up and make her wear a blindfold.

Then his hand on her ass moved to between her legs and rubbed against her clit. She widened her stance to allow him better access, and he pinched her sensitive nub. "Sean."

He pinched her again, and lights danced before her eyes before a wave of pleasure coursed through her body. She was barely aware of Sean still pounding into her until he stilled and gave a roar loud enough to be heard down the hall.

As the spasms of her pussy slowed, she murmured, "Hold me, Sean."

Never removing his cock, he gently lifted her torso off the couch until she was leaning against his chest. She looked up into his blue eyes and smiled. "Is roaring loud enough to wake the neighbors another shifter tradition?"

He chuckled before placing a gentle kiss on her lips. "I think the tradition decrees three orgasms loud enough to be heard down the hall."

"Decrees, huh?" He grinned and she couldn't help but soften against him. "I'm starting to like some of these obscure traditions. Why don't you teach me a few more of them tonight?"

His eyes turned heated. "Baby, I have a whole list of traditions to try with you."

He kissed her again, more demanding this time as his tongue swept her mouth. When he finally pulled away, she smiled and said. "Let's hope tonight is just the beginning. We have a whole lifetime to try them all. I'm sure they'll get pretty creative by the time we're fifty."

Sean laughed and the sound warmed her heart. Whatever troubles they would face in the future, and she knew there would be quite a few considering the nature of their marriage, she could handle any of it as long as she had this wonderful, funny, loving man at her side. "I love you, Sean Fisher."

He squeezed her tightly. "I love you, too, Lauren Spencer-Fisher. Now how about I show you how much?"

One of his hands moved to her clit, and he gave it a light brush, the sensation making her pussy throb again. "Hmm, I think that's a good idea. After all, we still have to make you roar two more times tonight."

His hands cupped her breasts. "Then we'd better get started."

He did exactly that, and it wasn't long before he'd roared all three times. In the end, they'd made it four, just to be safe.

Dear Reader:

Thank you for reading *Cougar's First Christmas*! Lauren and Sean will show up again in the future and you can see how they're doing. The next story is about Aidan and a human named Claire Davis and is called *Resisting the Cougar*. It's a full-length book and I'll share an excerpt with you so you can have a taste. But first, if you enjoyed Sean and Lauren's story, then considering leaving a review. Thank you!

Would you like to know when my next release is available? (And receive exclusive goodies and information too?) You can sign up for my newsletter at www.jessiedonovan.com/newlsetter.

Thank you for spending time with my characters. Turn the page for a glimpse of the next book.

With Gratitude,
Jessie Donovan

Resisting the Cougar
(Cascade Shifters #3)

President of an organization fighting for the right of shifters and humans to marry each other, Claire Davis needs the support of a local shifter clan or her cause is doomed. Even though she's human, she finds a way to reach out to the Clan DarkStalker cougar-shifters. Once she arrives on their land, she learns what it will take to garner their support and her life will never be the same.

As head sentry of Clan DarkStalker, Aidan Scott has more important things to do than fetch a human from a secret location. Only because he's loyal to his clan leader does he agree. Yet before long, the human female tempts him in a way he hasn't felt since his mate died five years ago.

In order to make the world a better place for humans and shifters, the pair must work together and avoid being caught by the authorities. What neither expected was to find their own happily ever after in each other.

Excerpt from *Resisting the Cougar* (Cascade Shifters #3):

CHAPTER ONE

Claire Davis adjusted the glasses on her nose and tried not to think about how she was lost in the middle of the cougar-shifters' land. Not lost in the sense she could stop at a gas station and ask for directions. Rather, she was lost in the middle of the damn Cascade Mountains with no cell service and no map.

So much for technology making life easier; it always failed when Claire needed it the most.

Pulling over to the side of the road, she put the car in park and laid her forehead on the steering wheel. If only she had thought of a back-up plan. Reading the directions earlier had made everything seem so simple. What she hadn't accounted for was the low-level fog a few miles back.

Think, Davis, think. She wasn't the head of the Shifter Equality Alliance by luck. Stubbornness was her middle name, and she wasn't about to give up. Especially since her upcoming meeting was important. No, scratch that, the scheduled meeting with the cougar-shifters was goddamn historical.

Kian Murray had invited her to DarkStalker's land through a human acquaintance they shared. Because it was illegal for her, or any human, to be on any shifter's land without the federal government's permission, she'd been given detailed directions to help hide her true destination. Once she reached the final location in the directions, a DarkStalker sentry, named Aidan Scott, would blindfold her and take her the rest of the way.

She'd made it to step number forty-three out of forty-five before the fog had prevented her from finding her next landmark. So close, yet so far.

The number of steps jogged her memory. Raising her head, she then switched on the interior car light and picked up her printed directions. Scanning the page, she reached the end. "Aha. I was right. I'm only a few miles from the final destination. Maybe if I honk my horn and sit here, the cougar-shifters will find me."

Since she was alone on a tiny mountain road, the noise wouldn't attract any humans. Only a fool would try driving these mountains in March with snow still on the ground.

Well, a fool or a woman on a mission. The Shifter Equality Alliance, or SEA, needed this meeting. Without the shifters' help, SEA's push to make shifter-human marriages legal was doomed according to every set of data analyzed in the last few months. Clan DarkStalker was her best chance at making that happen. She needed to make the meeting, at any cost.

Taking a deep breath, she pressed the horn and held it for fifteen seconds before releasing it.

Claire scanned her surroundings, but five minutes later, she was still sitting in her car with no cougar in sight.

If at first you don't succeed, try, try again. The saying might be childish, but it pretty much described how she'd run her life over the last five years.

Placing her hand on the horn, she geared herself for the noise and pressed down. Rather than make it a straight noise, she beeped the horn to "Row, Row, Row Your Boat." Maybe the kids' song would signal she wasn't a threat.

As she waited in silence again, she kept a look out for any cougars. Eventually, they had to find her.

Right?

She refused to think about the alternative.

COUGAR'S FIRST CHRISTMAS

~~~

Aidan Scott swished his tail as he paced back and forth in his cougar form, the snow crunching under his paws.

The human was late.

If it were up to him, he'd wait five more minutes and then return home. Humans were certainly not worth his paws freezing in the late season snow. Just because his animal-half could survive in the cold didn't mean he enjoyed it.

However, his clan leader, Kian, had chosen him for this special assignment and he would do anything for the alpha of the DarkStalker cougar-shifters. After all, Kian had been there when Aidan had needed him the most. Aidan wasn't about to repay the debt by abandoning his leader because of Aidan's own prejudice.

If his leader said the meeting with the human female was important, he would treat it as such. He only hoped the human wouldn't betray them. From his experience, they tended to be good at doing exactly that.

A loud noise echoed through the forest and he pushed aside everything to focus. Scanning from left to right, he didn't see anything in the trees apart from the other animals. If there was a threat, it wasn't immediate.

He was fairly certain the noise had been a car horn honking in the distance. Since no one stumbled into these mountains by accident or bothered to look for the best backcountry hikes during early spring, the sound was either the human female or one of the anti-shifter extremist groups.

Given that Clan DarkStalker was hiding a human female named Lauren on their lands, it could just as easily be the latter as the former. He needed to assess the possible threat.

Aidan picked his way through the forest, careful to keep to the shadows and the branches of the trees. Thanks to his tan hide blending in with the trees, no one on the ground would know he was there.

He was nearly to the single-lane road that wound through this section of the mountains when the horn blared again in some kind of rhythm. Thanks to his supersensitive hearing, the sound sent shivers of pain down his spine. It took everything he had to stay on the branch under his feet. The noisy intruder had to be on the road.

Reaching the edge of the woods, he surveyed the area to look for the car. However, a low-level fog had rolled in and he couldn't see anything more than a foot in front of his face.

Fucking fantastic. He'd have to go in blind.

Well, I've been meaning to brush up on my hunting skills anyway. I'll use this as an opportunity. I just hope the person doesn't run me over.

Aidan had no desire to be road kill.

After crawling down the tree, he kept his body low to the ground as he approached the road. No car headlights beamed nearby, nor did he hear an engine running. *Good.* That would make his plan easier.

Inch by inch, he crawled until he could smell the still-warm oil of a car engine. Two more feet, and he could make out the shape of a dark SUV. Shifting his weight, Aidan jumped to the roof of the car. Someone screeched inside. Every cell in his body itched to attack and protect the clan, but if the human female was inside the car, his clan leader would never forgive him.

He moved his head and peered inside the driver's side window. A brown-haired, plump female with glasses was leaning over her steering wheel, no doubt looking for something in the fog.

96

COUGAR'S FIRST CHRISTMAS

Since her description matched the female named Claire Davis in his assignment brief, he tapped his claws against the window. The human turned her green eyes to his face.

To her credit, she didn't scream or shout. Rather, her brows came together. She looked irritated.

As if she had the right to be irritated. She was the one who'd gotten herself lost and scared every creature in a five-mile radius.

Jumping off the roof of the SUV, Aidan decided enough was enough. He needed to shift, guide the human to his leader, and then move on to something better worth his time. Concentrating, he imagined his body changing shape.

~ ~ ~

Claire's heart was still beating a million times a minute as the amber-eyed cougar jumped down from the roof of her car. To say the big cat had scared her was an understatement.

However, as the cougar's paws became hands, his face changed into that of a human male, and his tail disappeared into his back, her brain blanked at the tall, naked, and very muscular man standing outside her car window.

Darting her eyes down, she confirmed that yes, he was indeed naked. Even in the cold, the rumor about shifters and their cock sizes seemed to be true.

Stop thinking about the shifter's cock. She wasn't a naïve shifter groupie; Claire knew full well how nakedness was dismissed without a second thought among shifter clans.

With one last long look of his chiseled abs and light spattering of dark and gray hairs on his chest, she met the shifter's eyes. In human form, they weren't amber but brown, and currently filled with irritation.

97

Flipping the key in the ignition once, she rolled down the window. "Hello. Are you Aidan Scott?"

The man growled. "That's all you have to say? You've been creating a damn ruckus for the last fifteen minutes. The animals in the woods must be terrified."

Remember, you need him to guide you to DarkStalker's land. Be nice to him. "Sorry, I was lost."

He grunted. Just her luck she'd be assigned a grumpy-ass shifter.

Thirty seconds ticked by in silence. The man didn't so much as shiver in the cold.

If the muscles and sneak attack hadn't already proven he was a soldier, the shifter's ability to withstand any circumstance without blinking an eye would've done it.

Another thirty seconds ticked by. She tapped a finger against the steering wheel. If he wasn't going to talk, then she would. "I apologized. If you're waiting for me to beg for your forgiveness, that's not going to happen, buddy."

As soon as the words left her mouth, Claire wished she could take them back.

She opened her mouth to try to soothe the situation, but the shifter male beat her to it. "I don't have time for your chatter. Grab your stuff and follow me."

The shifter male turned and walked away. After a quick glance to his round, firm ass, Claire scrambled to roll up the window. Picking up her duffel bag from the passenger seat, she climbed out of the car and locked it. The shifter was already more than fifteen-feet away. She muttered, "Slow down and give a girl a chance," as she half-ran to his side. By the time she reached him, she was a little out of breath. Fighting for shifter equality didn't leave a lot of time for exercise.

COUGAR'S FIRST CHRISTMAS

The shifter, who still hadn't confirmed he was Aidan, said, "We've wasted too much time with your antics. Try to keep up."

As their feet crunched in the snow of the woods, she eyed his bare feet. The cold had to be painful.

Normally, she'd hold back and be polite. Hell, how many politicians had she met in Olympia and convinced to support her cause? She could be proper and dignified if she tried. But considering the shifter male was walking stark naked next to her, she figured formalities were out the window. Before she could convince herself otherwise, she asked, "Are you really going to walk how ever many miles naked in the snow? Won't you catch a cold or pneumonia or something?"

Aidan's brown eyes glanced to her and then back in front of them. "I don't need your concern. I know what I'm doing."

She managed to keep her mouth shut. If the man wanted to freeze to death, then that was his prerogative.

Claire, however, dug out her gloves and put up the hood of her winter jacket. Rather than suffer the cold in silence, she tried talking again. "Even if you have super-shifter body heat and don't have to worry about pneumonia, I do. Please tell me there's a car nearby."

"You're the one who got lost. Both of us suffering in the cold is your fault."

She blinked. After so many years of dealing with passive-aggressive behavior in Seattle, Claire wasn't sure of how to deal with Aidan's straightforwardness.

Before she could think of a witty reply, Aidan stated, "I'm going to shift and guide you to where the car is. Stay quiet, just in case."

"In case of what? No one comes up here in March apart from shifters."

He finally turned his head to meet her eyes. "I've lived here my whole life and I know what I'm doing, so listen for once."

"For once? When have I—"

Aidan's shift stalled her words. Watching the process of a man's body shrink into one of a two-hundred pound cougar was something she had always wanted to see, ever since she was a little girl. The morphing of his head into a feline's skull, the tail coming from his back, and his hands and feet turning into paws was beautiful but had to be painful.

Maybe someday she would be able to ask if shifting hurt or not.

Aidan's amber cougar eyes met hers before he motioned with his head and started walking. As the male cougar tracked lightly through the snow, Claire rubbed her hands together and picked up her pace. If she didn't make the meeting with Kian Murray, she would definitely never have the chance to ask a shifter questions about their shifting process. As much as she didn't like Aidan's attitude, she followed his orders and walked in silence.

==================

Resisting the Cougar
Available Now in Paperback

For exclusive content and updates, sign up for my newsletter at: http://www.jessiedonovan.com

Author's Note

Thank you for reading my story. Writing is far from a solitary project and I wanted to thank a few people:

—Thank you to Virginia, Becky, and all the ladies at Hot Tree Editing. I appreciate all of your help in making my story shine. :)

—A huge, huge thank you to my cover designer, Clarissa Yeo of Yocla Designs. She makes the most amazing covers. Not only that, she doesn't so much as bat an eye when I ask for an interracial couple. Thanks Clarissa!

—A big thanks to Donna H. for her beta-reading comments. Without her, this story would be a whole chapter shorter!

And most of all, I want to thank you, the reader. I'm grateful for all my readers and fans, and I hope you join me over on my Facebook Author Page (facebook.com/JessieDonovanAuthor) to have some fun or just to drop me a line. I always respond!

Now, I'm off to write some more books…

About the Author

Jessie Donovan wrote her first story at age five, and after discovering *The Dragonriders of Pern* series by Anne McCaffrey in junior high, she realized people actually wanted to read stories like those floating around inside her head. From there on out, she was determined to tap into her over-active imagination and write a book someday.

After living abroad for five years and earning degrees in Japanese, Anthropology, and Secondary Education, she buckled down and finally wrote her first full-length book. While that story will never see the light of day, it laid the world-building groundwork of what would become her debut paranormal romance, *Blaze of Secrets*. In October 2014, she became a USA Today Bestseller.

Jessie loves to interact with readers, and when not traipsing around some foreign country on a shoestring, can often be found on Facebook and Twitter. Check out her pages below:

http://www.facebook.com/JessieDonovanAuthor
http://www.twitter.com/jessiedauthor

And don't forget to sign-up for her newsletter to receive sneak peeks and inside information. You can sign-up on her website:

http:///www.jessiedonovan.com

Made in the USA
Middletown, DE
29 September 2017